# "You may as well say it."

He wasn't going to let her avoid the discussion. "Or I might think you haven't decided to take control of your own life after all."

"Yes," she confessed, though it came out in a hoarse whisper.

His eyes flickered slightly. "Yes, what?"

"Yes, I still want you to make love to me."

Her satisfaction was strong as the words came out, steady and sure.

He held her gaze for ages, the silence in the car deafening.

"I'm not sure if you're still a fool, Audrey Farnsworth," he said at last, his voice low and almost angry, "or the most devious young woman I've ever met."

**MIRANDA LEE** was born and brought up in New South Wales, Australia. She had a brief career as cellist in an orchestra, and then another as a computer programmer. A move to the country after marriage and the birth of the first of three daughters limited her career opportunities to being a full-time wife and mother. Encouraged by her family, she began writing in 1982. She favors a well-paced what-happens-next kind of story, but says what matters most "is that my books please and entertain my readers, leaving them feeling good and optimistic about love and marriage in our present topsy-turvy world."

## Books by Miranda Lee

# MIRANDA LEE

## Knight to the Rescue

**Harlequin Books**

TORONTO • NEW YORK • LONDON
AMSTERDAM • PARIS • SYDNEY • HAMBURG
STOCKHOLM • ATHENS • TOKYO • MILAN
MADRID • WARSAW • BUDAPEST • AUCKLAND

ISBN 0-373-11702-7

KNIGHT TO THE RESCUE

Copyright © 1992 by Miranda Lee.

# CHAPTER ONE

AUDREY stood on the pavement outside the coffee-lounge, frowning as she glanced up and down the street. Russell was late. As usual.

She took a deep steadying breath and let it out slowly, willing herself to stay calm, not to become agitated.

You won't have to worry about his being late again after today, she told herself sternly. Russell will no longer be a part of your personal life.

But nothing could stop the pain deep down in her heart. Or the self-accusations.

Why did I get mixed up with such an obvious womaniser in the first place? she agonised. Why did I believe all his protestations of love? And why, oh, why did I let him talk me into going to bed with him?

Audrey suspected why as soon as she saw him striding down the street towards her, looking elegantly suave in a grey business suit. Russell had all the seductive trappings of a romantic charmer with his blond good looks and bedroom blue eyes, not forgetting his smooth line of patter which made him an excellent salesman.

When he'd started work with Modern Office Supplies as a representative a few months ago he'd been quite a hit with the office girls, yet within days he'd singled *her* out for his attentions.

Initially, she *had* been sceptical. After all, there were many more attractive girls at work. But he'd been so persistent, so seemingly sincere. And of course she'd been hopelessly flattered. What a naïve fool she'd been!

Audrey flicked an unhappy sideways glance at herself in the window glass next to her, almost flinching away from her reflection. She'd only had to take a good look in the mirror to realise that Russell couldn't have fallen in love so quickly with a girl as plain as herself.

Lord, how she hated her looks! Her white, white skin, her big doe-like brown eyes, her bow-shaped little girl mouth. As for her hair... It had always been a disaster. She had been born with fine mousy brown locks, but it was at present a burgundy shade, and permed into a bush of tight curls. Lavinia said it suited her. Audrey wasn't so sure. Neither did she feel comfortable wearing the red woollen dress her stepmother had given her, insisting red was one of her colours. *No* colour seemed to be her colour!

With a shudder, she returned her attention to Russell, who had put a wide apologetic smile on his face at his last stride.

'Sorry I'm late, darling,' he said silkily, and bent to give her a kiss on the cheek.

Audrey's whole insides twisted with dismay. How happy she had been the first time he'd called her that! Now, the word was like a dagger in her heart, a dagger dipped in treachery.

'Oh-oh.' Russell tried laughing on seeing her tight pale face. 'Methinks I've done something to put myself in your bad books. Is that why you asked me to meet you here for coffee this afternoon, to rap my knuckles over something? Or is the hang-dog face just because I'm a wee bit late?' he added, a caustic edge creeping into his voice.

How strange, Audrey thought. All of a sudden I don't find him that handsome, *or* charming. '*Half an hour* late, Russell,' she said coldly, 'is hardly a wee bit. I asked you to meet me at three. It's now nearly three-thirty.'

His shrug was dismissive, his smile trying in vain to melt the ice that was gathering around her heart. 'Yes, but I'm worth waiting for, aren't I?'

Audrey cringed. Had there been a time she'd actually *liked* lines like that? She could hardly believe herself capable of being such a mug. But she supposed unattractive girls were very vulnerable when it came to attentions from members of the opposite sex. Desperation, she decided bitterly.

'Do you think we could go inside and sit down?' she said sharply.

'Sure. I'll order us both cappuccino on the way in.'

The coffee-lounge was typical of a thousand others one would find in main streets in suburban Sydney—a long thin rectangle with booths along one side and a shiny counter stretching along the other. Audrey had thought that at this time on a Friday afternoon it would be practically empty and would give them some privacy. But this wasn't the case, with nearly every booth occupied. Only the back two were empty.

Audrey headed for the furthest, aware that her nervous tension was increasing with each second. The time for confrontation had finally come.

The second last booth was occupied after all, by a man bent over a newspaper. He glanced up briefly as she passed, but didn't take a second look.

Audrey sat down in the last booth with a weary sigh, then watched unhappily while Russell flirted with the girl behind the counter. The girl's eyes followed him hungrily when he turned and swaggered towards the back booth, a cocky grin on his face. More wool fell from Audrey's eyes. Was that how he got his kicks out of life? Making as many female conquests as he could? What number had *she* been? Ten? Twenty? A hundred?

He slid into the green vinyl seat opposite and shot her an expectant look. 'Well? Are you going to satisfy my curiosity and tell me what's up?'

'Yes,' she said stiffly, and dragged in a rasping breath. Her heart started hammering away in her chest, and when the words came out they were high-pitched and shaking. 'Diane told me today you took her out last Saturday night—the night you said you had a business dinner. She also said that you...you slept with her.'

Russell's instant scowl wiped every shred of good looks from his face. His top lip curled nastily and his eyes took on a narrowed, mean expression. 'So *this* is why I'm here! To answer a whole lot of stupid bloody accusations. I would have thought you'd have more sense than to listen to a silly bitch like Diane!'

'She wasn't lying,' Audrey said brokenly, upset by this further glimpse of the real Russell. He'd never used coarse words in front of her before. He'd always played the role of gentleman.

'Of course she was,' he sneered. 'She's jealous of you. If you had any brains you'd know that by now.'

Audrey sucked in a hurt breath at this further insult. But her pain only fired her with more resolution to be done with this man, once and for all. 'She had the motel receipt for last Saturday night,' she stated shakily but with determination. 'It's signed by you, and I . . . I know your signature.'

There was a short sharp silence, followed by an irritable sigh from Russell. 'Audrey . . .' he began in an impatient tone.

She lifted her chin and tried to still her quavering voice. 'There's no point in lying to me, Russell. We're finished, anyway.'

'You don't mean that.'

'I . . . I do. I believe Diane and I'll keep on believing her no matter what you say.'

'Is that so?' he muttered nastily. 'Well, in that case you might as well know. I did screw her. So what?'

Audrey could not contain the gasp of shock at this newly crude and callous Russell. Or the dismay that she'd actually allowed him to . . . to . . .

'You said you loved me,' she said in a dazed wretched voice. 'Wanted to marry me . . .'

'Yes, well, of course I did,' Russell retorted caustically. 'You're the big boss's daughter, aren't you? His *only* daughter. His only child, in fact. Do I have to spell it out any further?'

A groaning, whimpering sound escaped Audrey's lips before she could snatch it back. God, why hadn't she thought of that herself? There she'd been, assuming he was just a compulsive womaniser . . .

'You didn't mean *any* of it?' she said in a strangled tone. 'It was all just . . . for my money?'

His laugh was cruel. 'What's the problem, honey? Did you really think I was bowled over by your beauty and sex appeal? Oh, you're not that

bad-looking once you take off those ghastly clothes
you wear. But God, you've got no idea how to
please a man in bed. Audrey, dear, you're a bore!
I was doing you a big favour even taking you out,
let alone giving you a bit, but I suppose you won't
see it that way. I suppose you're going to run home
and tell darling Daddy that one of his big bad reps
seduced his prissy little virginal daughter.'

Revulsion had crept over her skin as she listened
to the ugly words spew forth. 'Don't worry,' she
choked out, and shuddered. 'I won't tell Father.'
God, she did have some pride left. Not much. But
enough to cling to and stop herself from falling into
the despair she could feel hovering at the edges of
her mind.

'Just as bloody well, because if you do and I get
the sack I'll make sure every man in the company
and the whole of damned Sydney knows just what
a vicious, vindictive bitch you are. And *don't* go
telling people in the office *you* broke up with *me*,
sweetheart. Not that they'd believe it. Hell, I can
have any bird I want. I just felt sorry for you, that's
all, thought I'd bring you out of your shell a little.
You should be grateful for small mercies instead
of...'

Russell raved on, but Audrey's mind was blocked
to his cruel and arrogant blusterings. She was
thinking bleakly about what happened to girls like
herself, girls who were unutterable failures where
men and sex were concerned, but who had the lure
of money. Girls like her own mother...

She closed her eyes against the agony of truth
that blasted into her brain. But along with the agony
came fury at a fate which would perversely make
a girl wealthy but plain, a girl who more than any-

thing else wanted a family of her own to love and cherish, who had dreamt of it for such a long long time.

Her fingers tightened around her handbag and she was about to sweep sideways out of the booth when someone moved abruptly into her path.

Startled, she glanced up a long long way to encounter a man of about thirty looming over her, an apologetic smile on his extremely attractive mouth. Dazzling white teeth gleamed in a deeply tanned face, intelligent grey eyes flashing beneath thick wavy hair as black as night.

But if she'd been startled by this man's sudden and very striking appearance, she was more than startled by the words he spoke.

'Audrey, honey,' he said in a rich male voice, 'I just couldn't wait outside in the car any longer. I know you said you'd handle things but it didn't feel right to me.'

As he spoke, those expressive grey eyes easily held her own astonished ones, an underlying steeliness compelling her to keep looking at him and say nothing to reveal that he was a perfect stranger to her.

Or was he?

There was something vaguely familiar about him, yet she couldn't place him. She frowned her confusion. Who on earth *was* he? How did he know her name? And why was he saying such extraordinary things?

Once he'd finished speaking directly to her, he released her eyes, swinging his gaze over to Russell, who was sitting there with his mouth gaping open in a most unattractive fashion.

'It's Russell, isn't it?' the stranger went on blithely, shocking Audrey further with his knowledge of Russell's name. Her lips parted on a gasp, bringing a hard darting glance from the stranger which had them snapping shut again.

'Sorry about this, old chap,' came more of his amazing speech, 'but these things happen. Audrey and I only met last Saturday night but it was love at first sight for both of us. I never believed in such romantic rubbish before, but I've had to revise my ideas on the subject, haven't I, Audrey, my sweet?'

Audrey, my sweet, was now so stunned she just sat there in numbed silence, doe eyes wide, bow-shaped lips pressed tightly shut to stop herself from totally resembling a flapping flounder.

Russell was similarly stunned, but not into silence. 'Audrey! Who *is* this man?' he demanded to know. 'God, don't tell me you've been seeing someone behind my back!' His eyes narrowed furiously. 'Why, you little hypocrite, I'll——'

'Audrey, you naughty girl,' the man cut in in a firm but drily amused voice, 'you haven't told him yet, have you?' His shrug was one of eloquent elegance, drawing Audrey's eyes to his unconventional but dashing clothes. Loosely fitting black trousers teamed with a black crew-necked jumper, tucked in, a fawn leather belt emphasising his trim hipline.

'Now isn't that just like her, Russell?' he was saying. 'She does so hate hurting anyone. Look, perhaps you and I should step outside while you say what you have to say. We both know how sensitive Audrey is and perhaps it's best we have this out man-to-man.'

Russell jumped to his feet, all fluster and bluster. Next to the stranger, he looked puny, which surprised Audrey since Russell was five feet eleven inches tall with quite a good build. But the man next to him must have been at least six-three or -four, his broad-shouldered, stronger frame dwarfing Russell's shorter, lighter body.

'There's no need for that.' Russell was clearly unhappy with his odds in a fight. 'I get the picture. Anyway, you're welcome to her. All the money in the world isn't worth having to scr——'

The stranger's left hand shot out and closed over Russell's left wrist, drawing Audrey's gaze to the long, strong fingers. Russell winced visibly as they closed tightly.

'I wouldn't say another word if I were you,' their owner warned in a quiet voice that was even more threatening than the loudest roar. 'I also suggest you take yourself far away from here very quickly, before I forget I'm a gentleman in the presence of a lady.'

Russell began to open his mouth, thought better of it, then snapped it shut. Giving Audrey a savage glance, he extricated himself from the booth and stormed out.

The stranger watched him go, a hard though satisfied smile pulling at his mouth.

'Who...who *are* you?' Audrey blurted out, relieved to at last be able to voice her inner turmoil and confusion. Only satisfaction at seeing Russell so rattled had kept her silent.

His smile softened as he slid into the U-shaped booth opposite her. 'A friend.'

She leant back against the green leather seat and stared at him. *Had* they met before? Could he be some business acquaintance of her father's? No, no, she dismissed immediately. She would *never* have forgotten this man. 'I don't know you,' she stated firmly, though there was a slight tremor in her voice.

'Ah, yes. Perfectly true.' He frowned and stroked his chin for a few seconds, before his face cleared to an expression of dry amusement. 'Would you believe it if I said I was your guardian angel come to life to save you from a dastardly villain?'

'You ... don't look at all like an angel,' she said, smiling at the thought that, dressed all in black, her rescuer looked more like a visitor from the opposite region.

His answering smile was devastatingly attractive and Audrey's stomach actually fluttered. 'What about a knight rescuing a fair damsel in distress?' he suggested, then chuckled.

'Why is that so funny?' she asked ingenuously before the penny dropped. Her smile faded immediately. 'Oh, I see ... it's because I'm hardly a fair damsel ...'

'Good God, Audrey,' he sighed, clearly exasperated with her. 'That's not it at all! It was because my name is Knight. Elliot Knight. Why *wouldn't* you qualify as a fair damsel? Hell, you have the most exquisite fair skin, the loveliest big brown eyes and an extremely kissable mouth.'

A startled shock sent her fingers fluttering up to cover her mouth. What did this man want from her, to make him use blatant flattery? Her confusion became total, and it brought bewilderment and panic. 'I ... I don't know who or what you are, or how you came to know my name and everything, but I ... I think I should be getting back to work!' Audrey picked up her bag and went to stand up.

'Don't be such a silly little fool!' he snapped, his harsh words making her slump back down on the seat, staring at him with wounded eyes.

His sigh was weary. 'I'm sorry... I didn't mean that the way it sounded. But damn it all, why go back to that office to a sniggering Diane? It's nearly four on a Friday afternoon. You're the boss's daughter. Give it a miss for the rest of the day. By Monday, your and Russell's break-up will be last week's news. Come back to my place for a drink and a sit by the fire, then later I'll drive you home. Come on, what do you say?'

She blinked over at him. 'How do you *know* all those things about me? About Russell? And Diane?'

Quite a few emotions flickered through those fine grey eyes. Frustration. Irritation. Then finally... a weary resignation.

'I was sitting in the next booth a while back,' he confessed with reluctance. 'I overheard your—er— conversation with your boyfriend. He infuriated me so much I decided to teach him a lesson.'

So *that* was why he'd seemed familiar! Audrey was almost relieved to find a logical explanation for the man's extraordinary knowledge. But then she realised all he had overheard, and an embarrassed heat flooded her cheeks. 'Oh, God,' she cried, and shook her head in shame.

'You didn't do anything to be ashamed of, Audrey,' he said softly. 'Clearly, you were in love with the man and thought he loved you back. The blame is all his, not yours.'

'Perhaps,' she murmured, thinking that such naïveté in a girl who would be twenty-one next week was inexcusable. Hadn't she long known she was unattractive to men? Why hadn't she stopped to wonder why Russell would single her out?

'You're well rid of him, Audrey,' her companion continued in the same gentle tone.

'I dare say,' she murmured, 'but it still hurts.'

'Yes,' he nodded. 'I know...'

The essence of real understanding in her rescuer's voice drew her thoughts away from Russell to consider exactly what Elliot Knight had just done for her. And she was deeply moved. Most men would have silently borne witness to her shame and even sniggered in contempt at her gullibility. But compassion had stirred this stranger to come to her aid. And oh, how gallantly he had done that, routing the enemy without her losing face and even trying to make her feel better with his flattery about her looks.

'You really are a knight in shining armour, aren't you?' she said, a tender light shining in her eyes as she gazed at him.

The compliment clearly rattled him for a moment.

'But you don't have to keep on rescuing me, Mr Knight,' she went on shakily. 'You've already done enough. I'm...very grateful to you.' She bit her bottom lip when tears suddenly pricked at her eyes.

'Come on...' He took her hand and slid out of the booth, pulling her with him. 'You're coming home with me for a while and that's final. I don't live far.'

'Oh, but I can't, Mr Knight. I...I...'

'Don't argue with me, Audrey. This is for your own good. And for pity's sake, call me Elliot! And before you ask, *no*, I'm not married. Neither do I have a girlfriend who might get the wrong idea. Does that settle all your doubts?'

Audrey might have resisted but in all truth she didn't want to go back to the office. Neither did she think Elliot had any dark sexual motive for taking her home. Not with *her*!

It wasn't till she was led over to the black Saab Cabriolet parked outside that she ground to a halt, wrenching her hand away from Elliot's solid grasp. '*This* is your car?' she asked, an instant quavering in her voice.

He frowned first at her, then at the car. 'Yes? Something wrong with it?'

'No... no, I suppose not,' she agreed stiffly, and with grim determination climbed into the sporty car. Nevertheless, an automatic tension took hold of her once the car started round the narrow winding cliff road that led from Newport to Avalon Beach, and Audrey wondered grimly if she'd ever get over this phobia.

She thought she managed to hide it quite well for the short trip, though she felt real relief when Elliot directed the car from the main road up a steep driveway. When he zoomed into an electronically operated garage underneath an impressively large ocean-view home and finally turned off the engine she let out a ragged, long-held breath.

He shot her a curious look and turned to pick up a newspaper that was lying on the back seat. 'You're a very nervous passenger.'

'Yes, I... speed makes me nervous,' she admitted. 'Men who own sports cars usually drive fast.

You don't, though. But then...you're different
from most men.'

'Really?' He laughed drily. 'I doubt that, Audrey.
I doubt that very much.' And lanced her with the
oddest look before abruptly turning away from her
to alight.

Her forehead puckered into a puzzled frown as
he guided her up the internal spiral staircase to
emerge on the lowest level of the split-level dwelling.
What had he meant by that remark, and that look?
That he was no better than Russell? That he might
consider seducing an heiress, even if she wasn't all
that attractive?

Even though she couldn't believe her shining
knight would do such a thing, Audrey's newly
cynical self still went on the alert.

But the sight of the huge living-room with its high
raked ceilings and wood-panelled walls reassured
her again, as did the furniture and rugs—all
valuable antiques. People didn't rent homes full of
such treasures, she decided logically. They owned
them.

'You must be very well off, Elliot,' she said, relieved eyes sweeping around in a full circle.
Goodness, if she wasn't mistaken that was a Renoir
on the wall. And a Gauguin! They didn't look like
prints, either.

'Very,' he agreed, striding across the room to
throw the newspaper on an ornate Edwardian coffee
table. 'Make yourself at home.' He waved towards
the brown leather studded sofa that faced the
fireplace.

'What exactly do you do?' she asked as she sat
down.

Elliot had moved over to the cold hearth of the marble fireplace when she threw this question at him. He sent her a wry glance over his shoulder then bent to put a firestarter into the dead ashes before arranging some kindling and firewood in a criss-cross pattern. 'What do I do?' he drawled as he struck a match. 'Let's see, now...'

He stood up and turned to face her, a sardonic smile on his face. 'Actually I haven't been doing much at all lately. I went skiing a fortnight back. Yesterday, I read a fairly good book. Tomorrow I'm going to try my hand at betting on the races.'

'Don't you *work*?'

'Shall we say, I have no need to unless I want to? And I haven't been wanting to this year.'

'Goodness,' she exclaimed, totally intrigued by him now. 'Were you *born* rich?'

'Not at all.' Elliot proceeded over to his built-in bar. 'What do you fancy? Gin? Vodka? A glass of white wine?'

'Oh—er—yes, white wine.'

He turned and extracted a bottle of Riesling from a wall fridge, opening it like a man who'd had a lot of practice. Pouring a glass each, he carried them over to the sofa.

Fascinated, her eyes followed his every move. He was so unconsciously graceful, yet so...masculine.

'The truth is,' he said as he handed over her glass and sat down in front of the crackling fire, 'I was once married to a rich woman.'

Shock sent her wine glass trembling, and wide eyes flashing to his. 'You mean you married a woman for her money?'

His self-irritation was obvious by the expression on his face. 'No, of course not. Please don't think that. I was merely explaining where a lot of my money came from. Moira died, you see. Late last year. Viral pneumonia,' he finished tersely before she could ask.

Audrey was taken aback that a person could die of pneumonia in the modern-day world of anti-biotics. And said so.

'My wife suffered from multiple sclerosis for some time,' he elaborated reluctantly, 'and had developed an aversion to doctors. I was away from home when she came down with what she thought was flu. Friends tell me she refused to call in a doctor. When I arrived home she was very ill. I raced her to hospital but she died within hours.'

'Oh, how awful for you, Elliot,' Audrey murmured.

He looked uncomfortable with her sympathy, his fingers tightening around his glass. 'Yes,' he said gruffly. 'Yes, it was.'

For her part, Audrey could not get out of her mind how devastating such a situation must have been. To have one's wife, or husband, snatched away so... unexpectedly young. But then, sudden death was always devastating. Nothing could ever prepare you for the gaping hole left in one's life when a loved one was wrenched away abruptly.

Audrey knew she was going to cry if she kept thinking on that subject. With an enormous strength of will, she pulled herself together, straightening her shoulders and taking a steadying breath. Only then did she notice Elliot was watching her very closely, a thoughtful expression on his face. Quite quickly she lifted her drink and took a sip, feeling embarrassed by his intense scrutiny.

'You ... didn't have any children?' she asked.

The muscles in his jaw clenched down tightly. 'No. Moira couldn't have any. Can we change the subject?' he demanded brusquely.

'Yes, yes, of course.' She felt guilty for having been so insensitive. Clearly he had loved this Moira very much. And was missing her terribly. Audrey fell awkwardly silent.

'Tell me about Russell,' he said at last.

A shudder went through her. 'Do I have to?'

'I think it might be a good idea,' he stated matter-of-factly. 'Perhaps I can give you a different perspective on the man, show him up for what he is. Someone not worthy of any heartache.'

'Believe me, I can see that already.'

'What about your father?'

She frowned. 'My father?'

'Did he know you were going out with this Russell fellow?'

Her chest tightened. 'Yes.'

'And he *approved*?'

She shrugged in an effort to ease her instant inner tension. 'He seemed pleased a man was taking some interest in me at last. My father is one of those men who thinks women are nothing if not married. He considers me prime spinster material,' she finished with a bitter laugh.

'That's rubbish on all counts! Women don't have to marry early these days. Or at all, for that matter. Either way, you're only a spring chicken.'

'I'm twenty-one next week.'

His laughter was dry. 'Positively ancient.'

'It is if you look the way I do. Lavinia always says that with money even the plainest girls can look good when they're young, but after a certain age it's downhill all the way.'

Audrey was startled by the look of sheer fury that flashed into his eyes.

'And who,' he ground out, 'is Lavinia?'

'My stepmother.'

'Your stepmother…' One of his dark brows lifted in a sardonic fashion. 'And your stepmother told you you were plain?'

Audrey saw what he was thinking now. That Lavinia was the hackneyed wicked witch of a stepmother. 'No, no, Lavinia wouldn't be that cruel. She's very nice to me. She tries awfully hard to help me with my hair and my clothes. But I'm a lost cause. Nothing seems to suit me.'

All the while she was talking, Audrey could see Elliot was not convinced.

'And how old is this stepmother of yours?' he probed, eyes unreadable as they flicked over her. 'The one who helps you with your hair and clothes.'

'She's in her late thirties. But she looks younger. She's very beautiful, and very confident in herself.'

An envious sigh escaped Audrey's lips before she could prevent it. But she did so wish sometimes that she could look even half as gorgeous as Lavinia could.

'I don't know where you got the idea you weren't attractive, Audrey,' Elliot pronounced.

An angry resentment flared within her. 'Please don't keep flattering me, Elliot. It's not necessary. I know what I am and I know what I look like.'

Suddenly there was no stopping the tears that had threatened all afternoon. They came with a rush, flooding her eyes, spilling down over her pale cheeks. Appalled at herself, she tried to choke back the sounds, to smother them by putting her wine glass down and dropping her face into her hands.

And she succeeded. But her shoulders still shook uncontrollably, and she had no idea how heart-wrenching the sight of her was, huddled there, crying silent bitter despairing tears.

'Audrey, don't,' Elliot groaned, and, putting his own glass down, gathered her into his arms. Quite automatically, her arms went round his securely solid chest to hug him with a desperate tightness.

When one of his hands lifted to stroke her hair, Audrey's response took her by surprise. Despite her distress, she thrilled to his touch and when he whispered sweet words of comfort she quivered with secret delight.

'You *are* nice-looking, Audrey. I *haven't* been flattering you . . .'

How did it happen, that moment when he tipped her tear-stained face up and bent his mouth to hers? Audrey froze for a second, but his lips were soft, soothing. Instruments of sweetness and sympathy. She sighed into them, her own parting, her arms creeping up to slide around his neck.

It was then that the kiss changed, that Elliot's mouth abruptly turned hard and demanding, his hands tightening around her. He forced her lips widely apart and his tongue drove deep.

A quiver of shock ran through Audrey's body and she began to struggle against him, her hands beating at his chest in a wildly flowering panic.

When he finally reefed backwards, her big brown eyes lanced his with shock and confusion.

He shook his head, his face filling with self-disgust. 'Oh, God . . . I'm sorry, Audrey. Terribly sorry.' His shrug was as weary and frustrated as his voice. 'I got carried away.'

'But...but *why*?' she choked out, staring at him. 'I mean...'

A black, sardonic grimace twisted his mouth. 'There's one more lesson you must learn today about men, Audrey,' he growled. 'When it comes to sex they're basically animals. Sometimes, they want what they want when they want it, and who they're having it with doesn't figure largely in their minds. I've been celibate now for nearly a year. Judging by what just happened, I think my monastic existence is about to come to an end.

'But not with you, my dear young girl,' he added, slicing her with a rueful look. 'Not with you... Come on. I'm taking you home.'

# CHAPTER TWO

MONDAY morning found Audrey in a turmoil. She didn't want to go to work, didn't want to face a sniggering Diane or a sulkily hostile Russell, didn't want to spend the day pretending everything was fine when it wasn't.

Slumping down on the side of her bed, she buried her face in her hands. But there were no tears left to be spilled. She'd cried herself out last Friday night, cried and cried till she was drained of tears, drained of energy, drained of all emotion.

Saturday she had spent in a deep dark depression, Sunday in an apathetic gloom.

Now, the working week was beginning and her life was going on, whether she wanted it to or not. She had no alternative but to pull herself together and get on with living. But before she could do that she had to face, once and for all, the truth behind what had happened last Friday.

Her head lifted from her hands, a confusing pain squeezing at her heart. Which had hurt her the most? she puzzled. Russell's betrayal? Or Elliot Knight's speedy defection?

She wasn't sure. She wasn't sure about anything any more. All she knew was what she had always known—or suspected—about herself. That she was a complete failure where men were concerned. Russell's only reason for making love to her had been greed, Elliot's pity. Not that his brief kiss could be termed 'making love'.

She would never forget his shock at his own behaviour. What on earth was he doing, he'd obviously thought, kissing this silly little nincompoop? And then getting carried away. No doubt he had to have been *very* frustrated at the time, Audrey decided bitterly. Nothing else could possibly explain a man like him turning uncontrollably passionate with someone like her. Russell had spelt it out. She had about as much sex appeal as a squashed frog!

Russell...

She could hardly bear to think of him, to think of what he had done. Or, more to the point, what she had allowed him to do. She was a fool—a stupid, naïve, plain, insecure little fool!

More desolation was about to sweep in when Elliot's compliments filtered back to her mind, the ones he'd insisted were sincere. He had said she had lovely skin, nice eyes and a very kissable mouth. *Had* he been merely flattering her, trying to make her feel better? Or could it be true? Her heart lifted a fraction. Even Russell had said she wasn't that bad looking.

She stood up and walked hesitantly over to the cheval mirror in the corner, her hand lifting to trace over her face and mouth as she stared into the mirror. In her opinion, her skin always looked too pale, her eyes too big, her mouth too little girlish. But yes...she supposed she wasn't really ugly. Merely colourless.

Her gaze lifted to her hair and she shuddered. Nothing colourless there.

Russell's hurtful comment about her clothes being ghastly jumped back into her mind and her eyes dropped to the hot pink suit she was wearing.

A frown creased her brow as she accepted that, while it wasn't exactly ghastly, it certainly didn't look good. Odd, because Lavinia had a similar suit—in red—and it looked great on her. Audrey knew her figure was not as spectacular as her stepmother's but it was still quite good. Slender, with enough curves in all the right places.

Her frown deepened in frustration. If only she had some fashion sense of her own, some confidence in her own judgement.

But she didn't. She never had had. She wished there were someone other than Lavinia whose opinion she could ask, someone mature and objective who would be totally honest with her. It worried Audrey that perhaps Lavinia was saying things looked nice on her simply because she didn't want to hurt her feelings.

Her mind slid, for the umpteenth time since last Friday evening, to Elliot Knight.

Elliot would tell her how it was. Elliot was honest, to the point of being blunt. Elliot...

He had driven her home in grim silence, depositing her on her doorstep with some very strong parting words.

'I refuse to apologise again for what happened, Audrey,' he said sharply. '*You* must take some of the responsibility. You're a grown woman, and it's about time you started acting and thinking like one. Firstly, in future don't go letting any personable stranger talk you into going back to his place as you did with me this afternoon. It's naïve and dangerous. Secondly, don't go to bed with any man unless you, yourself, want to go to bed with him. Thirdly, be your own person in every way. Form your own opinions about who you are and where you're going. You only have one life, Audrey. In the end, you're the one who has to live with your decisions. Make sure they *are* yours.'

He had gone to leave her, then added over his shoulder, 'I won't be calling you, Audrey. Don't take this personally. Any continuing friendship with me at this point in time is not in your best interests. Of course, if you're ever in any real trouble, please don't hesitate to ring and I'll help in any way I can.'

Audrey sank down on the end of her bed with a sigh. She had to admit that wanting some advice about fashion hardly constituted *real* trouble. Not that she would dare ring him anyway. Quite frankly, she wouldn't have the nerve. Just thinking about Elliot answering in that unswervingly direct voice of his made her quiver. In fact, thinking about Elliot at all was proving unnerving.

Her stomach curled as she recalled how it had felt when he'd kissed her, when his tongue had thrust deep into her mouth. Her heart had leapt madly, and the blood had roared around her head for a few seconds. At the time, she had been stunned by the raw sexual desire that had flared within her. She had never felt anything like it with Russell. Even now, just thinking about it sent her into a spin. She kept wondering what would have happened if her shock hadn't made her struggle, if Elliot hadn't stopped.

The thought started her heart racing. Audrey strongly suspected that it was these intense physical reactions Elliot could evoke in her—not so much Russell's treachery—that had caused her such distress on Friday night. She'd been upset because she had not wanted Elliot to take her home. She had wanted him to take her to bed. There! She had admitted it. In fact, if she didn't know better she might believe she had fallen out of love with one man and fallen in love with another in a single afternoon! Which was crazy!

Though perhaps not so crazy, Audrey conceded, if she had never been in love with Russell in the first place. Perhaps she'd merely been attracted to his good looks, flattered by his attention, seduced by his lies. Silly little Audrey, craving love, desperate to believe *any* assertions of affection. She shuddered as she recalled all his lies whenever he'd coaxed her into bed. Clearly he'd been laughing at her the whole time.

And rightly so, she decided wretchedly. She was a gullible young idiot. She was still being an idiot, imagining she was in love with another man now, just because he had aroused her with a passionate kiss.

Audrey shook her head in dismay. Dear me, when was she ever going to grow up and see things as they really were, and not as her romantic heart wanted to see them? Elliot was a handsome, sexy, sophisticated man who had acted gallantly towards her, then stirred her with a kiss at a vulnerable moment. That didn't mean she was in love with him. Infatuated, perhaps. That was all.

But if she wasn't in love with Elliot, why did the thought of never seeing him again produce such wrenching feelings inside her? Such black despair?

Audrey jumped to her feet, infuriated with herself. She was sick of feeling down, sick of self-pity, sick of romantic confusions and delusions. You're young and healthy and not *that* bad looking, she told herself sternly. You'll find someone to really love you one day, someone you'll love back, without doubt, without distress. Now stop moaning and groaning and get down to breakfast!

Her father was already in the sun-room that served as a breakfast-room, devouring his habitual steak and eggs, when she made an appearance. Elsie was standing at his shoulder, refilling his coffee-cup.

'Good morning,' Audrey said with determined brightness as she pulled out a chair at the circular table. 'Just coffee and one slice of toast for me, Elsie.'

'Righto, lovie.' Elsie waddled off. Having been a cook all her life, Elsie had sampled a few too many of her own makings. But she was a sweet old dear, without a mean bone in her body. Audrey was very fond of her.

Warwick Farnsworth looked up at his daughter with a reproachful frown on his face. 'You're not going to become one of those anorexics, are you, Audrey?'

She glanced across the table at her father and conceded that at fifty he was still a handsome man. Broad-shouldered and fit as a fiddle, he had thick brown hair, elegantly greying at the temples, and sharp blue eyes. For a brief moment, Audrey wished she'd inherited a few of his genes.

But not his lack of tact.

He had no idea how to relate to his daughter as a parent. Most of his conversations with her started with an exasperated-sounding question.

'I'm not anorexic, Father. I'm five feet four and weigh eight stone two. That's exactly what I should be.'

Audrey had learnt to answer her father with facts. He was a 'facts' man.

'Hmph!' he pronounced and picked up his coffee-cup, turning to flip open the morning paper next to him to the business section.

Elsie arrived with the toast and coffee, and Audrey settled down to spreading margarine and jam. Once her father had his nose in the newspaper, all conversation ceased. Which meant she was surprised when he suddenly spoke up again.

'You do realise, Audrey, that Lavinia is going to a lot of trouble for your birthday on Friday night?'

Audrey tried not to have ungrateful thoughts. Shy in any social situation, she had requested no celebration at all, but Lavinia had insisted on a dinner party with some people from work. Audrey had only given in graciously when Russell had liked the idea.

'She's been a good stepmother to you,' her father went on. '*Very* good. Even in the beginning, when you were hardly welcoming. She never once lost patience with you, despite your uncooperative, sullen disposition at the time.'

*Sullen?*

Resentment flared within Audrey. Hardly sullen. In pain maybe, from her own injuries from the car accident that had also claimed her mother. Two badly broken legs took a long time to heal. Not to mention her emotional pain of losing a mother she adored. But of course her father wouldn't understand that. He'd shown how insensitive he was by remarrying within six months of his wife's death.

With a clarity that had previously eluded her, Audrey finally accepted the rumours she had heard all her life and had blindly denied to herself. That her father had not loved her mother; that he had married her for the company.

She glared over at her father, recognising in him a man similar to Russell, a ruthlessly ambitious and mercenary man who had little love to give. He probably didn't even really love Lavinia. She was merely a decorative hostess, a beautiful and convenient body to have in bed, a possession, much like the paintings and sculpture he'd started collecting recently.

What annoyed Audrey even more was that, despite finally recognising her father's failings, she still loved him.

'Lavinia tells me you've cancelled your invitation to Russell for the dinner party,' he rapped out. 'Is that correct?'

'Yes.'

'Why?'

Her heart began thudding. 'We split up.'

'*Why*?' he insisted on knowing.

She was about to make some feeble excuse when something—some indefinably rebellious surge—made her say, 'I met someone else.'

Her father's face showed astonishment. 'You did? Who?'

Audrey gulped. Now she had done it. 'You...you don't know him.'

'Well, what's his name? Where did you meet him? What does he do?'

'I—er—his name is Elliot Knight. He lives at Avalon Beach and he's a man of independent means.' She wisely decided not to answer the question about where she'd met him. She didn't think her father would appreciate her saying Elliot had picked her up in a coffee-lounge.

'He's rich, you mean.'

'Yes, I guess so.'

'And he's still interested in you.'

Audrey's dismay was intense. So her father had known Russell was only interested in her money. And yet he had allowed the liaison to continue, knowing this all the time. Her sense of self-worth began to shrivel again. No man had *ever* been interested in her for herself alone. The only real emotion she'd managed to inspire in a man was pity. It was pity that had made Elliot come to her rescue, take her home, kiss her. Pity...

She wanted to cry with despair but her father was staring at her and some new strength—born of her recent bitter experience perhaps—kept her chin up, her eyes steady, forced her to say, 'He's *very* interested.'

'Then why don't you invite *him* to your party?'

'Invite who?' Lavinia asked as she swanned in in her favourite black satin négligé. Tall and voluptuous, with long wavy black hair flowing out over her shoulders, she was a striking and sensuous figure.

'Morning, darling.' She bent to kiss her husband's forehead before drifting over to pour herself some coffee from the percolator on the sideboard.

Audrey stared after her with undeniable envy. Oh, to be so elegant, so sure of oneself, so darned sexy!

'Audrey has a new boyfriend,' her father announced with a mixture of surprise and fatherly pride. 'She says he's *very* interested in her.'

Audrey winced. Now she was well and truly in the soup.

Lavinia whirled to stare disbelievingly at her. 'Really? Anyone we know?'

'I've already asked that. She says not. A wealthy young playboy from the sound of things.'

'But how would Audrey meet someone like that?' Lavinia scoffed. 'She never mixes in the social set around Sydney. Not that she shouldn't. She just never bothers with that scene. Are you sure she's telling the truth about all this? It all seems very odd.'

Audrey detested it when her father and Lavinia started talking around her. Normally, she either stayed unhappily silent or drifted away. But not this morning. 'Why on earth would I lie, Lavinia?' she challenged.

'Why, indeed?' the woman murmured.

'I'm only too happy to tell you about Elliot. You only have to ask.'

Lavinia lifted her finely arched dark brows and walked indolently back to sit down with her coffee. 'Well?' she prompted. 'Tell us, then. Where did you meet?'

Audrey swallowed, her newly discovered courage faltering. 'I—er—I . . .'

The sardonic light in Lavinia's black eyes forced Audrey to gather every available resource she owned. 'We met at a party last Saturday night,' she said, using Elliot's own white lie to Russell. 'Not the one just past. The weekend before.'

'But you didn't go out that night,' Lavinia pointed out.

Audrey's memory did a frantic data-search. Her father and Lavinia had gone out to a club that night. They hadn't come home till after midnight and certainly wouldn't have checked her room to see if she were in. Elsie was the only live-in servant and she always went to bed early.

Despite a pounding heart she managed a passably nonchalant shrug. 'I wasn't going to, but after you both went out an old schoolfriend of mine rang out of the blue and asked me to a flat-warming party. I'm certainly glad I went. Elliot's a fascinating man.'

Lavinia was not about to let up. 'If this Elliot's so interested in you, why did he let you spend the whole of this last weekend moping in your room? Why didn't he take you out?'

Audrey's stomach was beginning to churn. 'He went skiing. I . . . I didn't want to go. I hate skiing.'

'Looks like Audrey's come up trumps at last,' her father said, undeniably impressed. 'Are we to hope for an announcement in the near future?'

Audrey blushed. 'Really, Father. We've only just met.'

'Fair enough. So when will he be back from skiing, this Elliot of yours?'

'Today,' she answered with astonishing glibness. There was no doubt lying came easier with practice. 'Late this afternoon.'

'Then you'll be able to ring him tonight,' Lavinia inserted smoothly, 'and ask him to your party.'

'Oh, but I . . . but surely . . .'

'Come now, Audrey!' Her father's tone showed exasperation. 'It's quite permissable for a girl to ring a boy these days. And after all, it *is* your coming of age. I'm sure this young man won't think you're chasing him, asking him to a twenty-first.'

Audrey groaned silently. Next thing they'd both stand over her while she actually made the call.

'Of course, if you don't think this Elliot will come,' Lavinia drawled.

Audrey stared at her stepmother. Strange, she'd always thought Lavinia liked her. But it was impossible to ignore the malicious gleam in those black eyes, or the smug sarcasm in her voice. It sparked a fierce determination Audrey hadn't known was in her.

'He'll come,' she bit out. 'Don't you worry about that.'

Lavinia's smugness wavered and Audrey felt an uncustomary thrill of satisfaction. She'd get Elliot to come if it was the last thing she did. She'd beg. She'd bribe. And if all that failed she'd lie her teeth out.

It was amazing how ten hours' delay could undermine one's resolve. By the time Audrey reached for her bedside phone early that evening her hand was literally shaking. Snatching it back, she sank down on her quilt and stared once again at the open telephone directory on her pillow, at the circled name.

KNIGHT E H. The only E Knight in the book living in the suburb of Avalon. It had to be him.

Taking another fortifying breath and trying to steady her hand, she reached for and picked up the phone, punching in the numbers with sharp, staccato movements. The nerve-racking *brr-brr* started on the other end of the line.

Would he be home at six on a Monday night? Audrey thought anxiously as the ringing continued. She had reasoned he should be. It was too early to go out to dinner and late enough to have come home if he'd gone out for the day. It was dark at six in July in Sydney, winter well and truly set in. With each successive ring, her agitation increased. One part of her wanted him to answer. The other hoped he'd gone to Switzerland for the rest of the winter.

On the seventh ring, someone answered.

Audrey held her breath.

A male voice repeated the number she had just rung.

She expelled the held breath in a rush. 'El . . . Elliot?'

There was a short sharp silence that sent Audrey's tension up and off the scale.

'Audrey? Is that you?' he questioned with a manner that suggested he was not pleased she had rung.

This was no less than she had expected. 'Yes, it's me,' she said, and fell painfully silent.

'Well?' he prodded at last. 'What can I do for you?' His tone was cool and she suddenly realised she was about to make a big fool of herself. Yet to fail was unthinkable. She just couldn't face Lavinia with the news that Elliot wasn't coming.

'I . . . I have this problem.'

'Yes?'

God, he wasn't making it easy for her, was he?

More feelings of pre-emptive failure flooded in, totally swamping her. He was going to say no. Why should she humiliate herself by asking in the first place?

Her heart turned over in wild desolation. If only she were beautiful and sexy. If only Elliot wasn't rich, and needed her money—like Russell. If only there were some way she could make him genuinely *want* to come.

'You . . . you said I could call if I needed help.'

'Yes?'

'I . . . I do.'

'In what way?'

Audrey took a deep breath. And the plunge. 'Remember I mentioned I was turning twenty-one soon? Well, it's this Friday and Lavinia has organised a special dinner party for me that evening here, at home. I was going to bring Russell, you see, and now I don't have anyone to be my date and I thought that...that... Well, I hoped you might fill in in Russell's absence.'

She held her breath and waited for his answer.

'I thought I made it clear, Audrey,' he ground out, 'that I'm not in the market for *filling in* for Russell, in *any* capacity.'

Audrey was glad Elliot couldn't see the heat zooming into her cheeks. She wished he hadn't used quite those words. It sent the most amazingly explicit and arousing images to her mind.

'Isn't there anyone else you can invite?' His tone was frustrated. 'Someone your own age?'

'Not really,' she replied, making a huge effort to get a hold of herself. 'No one I'd be proud of. And Elliot, I want to be proud of my date, don't you see? It's...it's very important to me.' Audrey knew this final plea was hitting below the belt. Out of desperation she was deliberating playing on Elliot's capacity for compassion.

His sigh was one of weary resignation. 'Yes, I do see. Unfortunately... Very well, Audrey. Give me your address and tell me what time I'm expected. And perhaps your last name might be a good idea. I never did find that out.'

Success brought both triumph and a measure of agitation. He was coming. He was actually coming. Shivers of unbidden excitement ran up and down her spine.

Audrey somehow managed to give him her home address at Newport, her full name of Audrey Henrietta Farnsworth, as well as her phone number—just in case a disaster prevented his coming. But please, lord, no disasters, she prayed!

'Could you be here soon after seven?' she requested breathlessly. 'We're having drinks before dinner. Oh, and wear a dinner-jacket. It's formal.'

When he hesitated again, she said worriedly, 'You do have a dinner-jacket, don't you?'

There was a smile in his voice when he answered. 'Yes, Audrey, I have a dinner-jacket.'

'I thought you might. Considering...'

'Considering what?'

'Considering you're rich and...well...obviously given to socialising.'

'I haven't been doing much of that lately,' he muttered. 'Perhaps I should have. And what are *you* going to wear, Audrey? Does formal mean a long dress?'

'Long dresses are out at the moment. Calf-length are in. I'm not sure what I'll wear yet. I was going to go shopping with Lavinia on Thursday after work. I'll probably end up buying something glitzy. Lavinia says glitz is definitely in.' Audrey stopped to draw breath. She knew she was babbling, but nerves affected her that way sometimes.

'Has it ever occurred to you that what's *in* might not suit you?' came his drawled remark. 'Or that Lavinia might choose something that suits her, not you?'

'Yes,' she confessed. 'That has ocurred to me, actually.'

'Well, why not buy something all by yourself, something *you* like?'

This idea still flustered her, because she truly had no confidence where her own taste was concerned. 'I'd like to,' she said unhappily. 'The trouble is I...I'm never sure what to buy. The sales ladies tell you *everything* looks nice and in the end I feel totally confused. I bought an evening dress by myself not long ago and Lavinia said it was a disaster. Totally lifeless and dreary on me.'

'What colour was it?'

'Plain cream, in a sort of silk material.'

'And the style?'

'Nothing spectacular. Long tight sleeves, fitted bodice, boat neck, lowish back. The skirt flares out.'

'Do you still have it?'

'Y...yes, but——'

'Let me make a suggestion,' he cut in forcibly. 'Wear it! Cream sounds a perfect colour for you. Put your hair up and wear plain gold earrings. No other jewellery, not even a watch. Neutral shades around your eyes. Plenty of blusher. Bronze lipstick and nail polish. Got that?'

'Well, yes...but...but...what *are* you,' she asked with a nervous laugh, 'an expert on women's fashions?'

'No. An expert on women.'

Her heart skipped a beat. She didn't doubt him for a moment.

For the first time Audrey wondered about the past women in his life. First his old girlfriends. Then his wife, Moira... Had she been beautiful? Sexy? Sophisticated? Had he loved her to distraction?

Of course, shot back the answer.

Audrey was startled by the intense jab of jealousy this thought brought. She hadn't really felt jealousy when she'd found out about Diane and Russell. Only pain at what his disloyalty revealed about herself, that she was incapable of inspiring a true and deep love. Yet with Elliot she was torn with envy to think of his even being with another woman, let alone loving her.

Did that mean she *had* fallen in love with him?

She hoped not. She really hoped not. The likes of Russell were easy to get over. Elliot was a different kettle of fish entirely. A man like him came along only once in a girl's lifetime and would be impossible to forget.

'Now promise me you won't let Lavinia dress you,' he was saying. 'That you'll do what I said.'

'I promise. And Elliot...thank you...'

'Don't mention it.'

He hung up and Audrey was left clasping the receiver to her ear. Her hand began to shake as she lowered it slowly on to its cradle. Friday... It seemed a million light years away.

# CHAPTER THREE

'MAY I come in, Audrey?'

'No, no, Lavinia, don't come in. I'm still getting dressed. I don't want anyone to see me till I'm all ready.'

'Really, all this mystery!' Lavinia said peevishly through the door. 'First you won't tell us anything about this Elliot you've invited. Now you won't let me see what you look like. I just thought you might need some help with your hair. After all, you didn't go to the hairdresser's with me this afternoon, even though your father arranged for you to have time off work.'

'My hair's fine,' she called back. 'I did it myself.'

'That's what I'm afraid of, dear. You know how——'

'Lavinia!' Audrey burst out with uncharacteristic assertiveness. 'Just leave me be for once!'

'You don't have to take that tone with me, Audrey. Truly, I don't know what's got into you today. Turning twenty-one is not a licence to be rude!'

Guilt assailed Audrey as she heard Lavinia flounce off, muttering. The impulse to go after her, call out, say something placatory was strong. But she was afraid Lavinia would say something patronising about her appearance, undermining the pleasurable confidence that was growing in Audrey every single second.

42

She turned to stare at herself in the full-length mirror one more time. She could hardly believe how good she looked. The cream silk dress didn't water down her fair complexion as Lavinia had said it would. It gave her skin a softly glowing sheen. The evidence before her eyes suggested to Audrey that the bright reds and pinks and purples Lavinia had been encouraging her to wear—supposedly to put colour in her face—had been having the opposite effect, making her looked washed-out and sickly.

As for her hair... Audrey had never felt entirely comfortable with either the burgundy colour or the tightly curled perm which fluffed it out every which way. But Lavinia and her hairdresser had insisted on both, saying her natural brown hair was thin and mousy, that her small face needed dramatic balance, whatever that was. Despite some misgivings, she had taken their advice because they were the experts, and to give them the benefit of the doubt it *was* a common enough style and colour these days. Audrey had seen it to good effect on other women.

But obviously not on her.

Now that she had put it up, suppressing the mass into a tight chignon, with only a few curls escaping, Audrey could see that a shorter, less bulky style would suit her heaps better. Maybe a lighter, softer colour would be better too. She resolved to do something about both as soon as possible.

The faint bong of the grandfather clock in the foyer striking seven filtered upstairs. Audrey swallowed, a burst of nerves fluttering into her stomach. Elliot would be arriving any minute, along with the other guests. She really should be going downstairs.

Still she dithered, terrified that someone would say something critical about how she looked. It wouldn't take much to shatter her new and fragile confidence. Maybe she didn't look as good as she thought. Maybe she was being deceived by a minimal improvement from her previous horror.

But it wasn't just her own appearance that was making her nervous. Elliot's would come as a bit of a shock, too. Both her father and Lavinia were probably picturing an effete and unprepossessing young snob, not the mature dashing figure Elliot would cut in a dinner suit. She hoped they wouldn't appear too astonished, or ask too many awkward questions. Elliot had no idea he had been cast in the role of ardent admirer. No doubt he imagined he was coming merely as a friend.

Quelling another flutter of nerves, Audrey took one last look in the mirror for renewed confidence and reluctantly made her way downstairs.

'Why, Audrey, my dear!' her father pronounced in surprised tones when she finally appeared in the doorway of the huge living-room. 'You look lovely! Doesn't she look lovely, Lavinia?'

Audrey's chest swelled, then tightened as Lavinia turned from where she was checking the glasses and decanters in the cocktail cabinet. Her black eyes narrowed as they travelled down then up the cream dress. 'Yes…quite lovely,' she agreed. But her eyes were angry.

Audrey was once again taken aback by her step-mother's attitude towards her, till she decided Lavinia's nose was out of place that her judgement about the cream dress had been wrong. No one liked to be shown up, but one would have thought she'd be pleased her stepdaughter looked nice for her own birthday party.

The front doorbell ringing distracted Audrey from her puzzled hurt.

Elliot! she thought breathlessly.

'I'll answer that, Maree,' she called out, stopping the maid in her tracks as she hurried across the black marble foyer towards the front door. The young woman, who'd been hired just for the night, looked hesitant for a moment, before making a shrugging retreat.

Audrey's heart was thudding loudly as she spun away from a sour-faced Lavinia and hastened to the front door. It wasn't Elliot, however. It was Edward Hurley and his wife, Alice. Tall and forty-ish, Edward was the sales manager for Modern Office Supplies Ltd, and Audrey's boss. Her gaining the position as his secretary over Diane was one of the reasons behind the other girl's jealousy. But Audrey knew she was a more efficient and better secretary than Diane and had never felt the position had gone to her merely through nepotism.

'My, my,' Edward murmured as his wide-eyed gaze ran over her, 'you're looking surprisingly *soignée*, Audrey. I hardly recognised you for a second.'

'You do have a habit of giving backhanded compliments, Edward,' his nice wife reproved. 'But that dress does suit you, Audrey. I love your hair up. It brings attention to your lovely eyes and skin.' Alice smiled and gave her a kiss on the cheek. 'Happy birthday, my dear. I hope you like this little gift,' she said, and pressed a small but beautifully packaged parcel into Audrey's hands.

'I'm sure I will,' Audrey beamed, buoyed up by the woman's warm and seemingly sincere compliments. Lavinia's uncharitable reaction to her improved appearance didn't hurt quite so much now. 'Here, let me take your coat.'

She had barely done as much when the doorbell rang again.

'That'll be Dwight,' Edward said. 'He pulled into the drive just as we reached the top step. As you can imagine, we decided not to wait for him.'

Audrey conceded that mounting the front steps at the Farnsworth residence took some time, since there were thirty of them. The house was relatively new and, Audrey thought, far too ostentatious. Double-storeyed, but of no particular style, it had columns and curlicues all over the place, not to mention acres of Italian marble and huge open-planned rooms that gave no sense of privacy.

She infinitely preferred the older, cosier home that had been her mother's family residence. But no sooner had Lavinia become the new Mrs Farnsworth than she had insisted on having a house built to her own taste. Audrey had come home one summer holiday from the boarding-school she'd been dispatched to, to find they had moved into this brand new edifice.

She turned again and opened the door a second time. Dwight Liston, Modern Office Supplies' sleek yuppie marketing manager, and his attractive blonde wife, Frances, literally gaped when they saw her. Their reaction did wonders for Audrey's growing self-esteem. But nothing could obliterate the underlying feeling of apprehension at Elliot's non-arrival. She threw an encompassing glance over her guests' shoulders at the driveway and the street beyond the garden wall. There wasn't a black Saab in sight. Surely, oh, surely he wasn't going to let her down!

Dwight and Frances were duly ushered inside along with Edward and Alice, their presents deposited on the special table alongside the very ornate birthday cake Lavinia had chosen. Audrey was vaguely conscious of several more lavish compliments on her appearance and a glass of champagne being pressed into her hands. But her smile was plastic, her ears straining to hear the thrum of Elliot's car arriving. When the maid offered her an hors-d'oeuvre she took it and ate it without having any idea what it was.

Since she didn't hear the sound of any car arriving, the sudden jangling of the doorbell snapped her head around. 'I take it you want to answer that too, Audrey?' Lavinia said caustically.

'I—er—yes, I do.' She plastered a wide smile on her face, still confused by her stepmother's new attitude. 'It must be Elliot, since he's the only one not here yet.'

As she put her glass down and hurried from the room she heard Edward say, 'Elliot? Who's Elliot? I thought Audrey was going out with Russell.' Apparently, office gossip hadn't reached management yet about her and their top sales representative being a past item. Diane had been smugly tight-lipped all week. On the one occasion Russell had been obliged to come into the office for a meeting, he had avoided Audrey like poison.

Not that she gave a hoot about either Diane or Russell at that moment. Relief was mingled with an escalating excitement as she swept to the front door. Nothing, however, could have prepared her for the feelings she had when she opened it.

Elliot stood there in an elegant black tuxedo, looking far more devastatingly handsome than she had remembered, and with the most enormous sheaf of creamy yellow roses in his arms. Audrey simply stared, first at the flowers, then at him. For what seemed a long long moment he stared back, his face quite unreadable.

His smile, when it came, was lop-sided and very droll. 'There must be a career for me somewhere as a make-over man,' he said drily. 'Audrey, you look simply stunning.' Bending forward, he gave her a peck on her cheek. 'Happy birthday, Cinderella.'

Emotions continued to bombard her heart, not the least an overwhelming gratitude. 'Oh, Elliot,' she choked out. 'Thank you. For coming. For...everything.' Tears pricked her eyes.

'If you cry,' he warned darkly, 'I'm going to walk back down those stupid damned steps this instant. Which is no mean feat. Who designed this monstrosity of an entrance, anyway? A mountain climber?' He stepped inside, closed the door behind him, then held out the roses.

She didn't cry. She laughed. With an uncharacteristic recklessness. Elliot, her friend, had come to her rescue again. She would accept his kindness once more; appreciate it; even enjoy it. She steadfastly refused to let any other feelings she had for him spoil her evening.

Taking the roses, she hooked her free arm through his left elbow and led him swiftly inside for all her guests to see, pausing with theatrical presence in the wide archway, flowers on one arm,

Elliot on the other. 'Everyone,' she announced, 'this is Elliot.'

Everyone was tellingly silent. All the men's eyes narrowed assessingly while their wives simply stared. Lavinia's shocked gaze recovered first to move over Elliot's superb and elegantly clad body in a blatantly sexual scrutiny.

Audrey's hold tightened on Elliot's arm as a stab of irrational fear shot through her.

*You can't have him*, her eyes and mind projected fiercely towards her stepmother.

Lavinia's eyes snapped her way, looking right through her before returning to Elliot, not so hungry this time, but still with undisguised interest.

Logic was slow to intervene, but even when it did Audrey's unreasoning panic took time to recede. Lavinia was a happily married woman, she reasoned. Not once, in the nine years she'd been Mrs Warwick Farnsworth, had Audrey seen her do more than casually flirt with a man. Surely she wouldn't set out to deliberately seduce her step-daughter's supposed boyfriend. Lavinia might be a bit of a bitch, Audrey decided, but she wasn't *wicked*.

'So this is Elliot,' Lavinia said, gliding forward to hold out a limply elegant hand. 'I can't say we know a lot about you. Audrey has been stubbornly secretive about her new admirer.'

Audrey felt the stiffening in Elliot's arm at this description of himself. Oh, dear, she almost panicked, and looked down.

'And you must be Lavinia,' Elliot returned suavely, dropping her hand after a cursory shake. 'I can't say the same for you. Audrey's been very vocal on what a wonderful stepmama you've been to her, haven't you, darling?'

Audrey was startled by the endearment so smoothly delivered. Then deeply touched. She swallowed and turned an adoring face up at him. Oh, you kind, kind man! she thought with heart swimming.

Although he smiled back down at her, Audrey had the impression that he was momentarily disconcerted. For a split second, as she looked at him, a worried light had gleamed deep in his fine eyes. But he quickly resumed his nonplussed air.

Lavinia looked definitely uncomfortable. She was used to compliments about her beauty, not her mothering abilities. No compliment about her beauty, however, was forthcoming, despite her looking quite breathtaking in a royal-blue crêpe dress with a heavily beaded matching jacket.

Instead, Elliot took Audrey's spare hand, holding her out at arm's length. 'Doesn't my girl look gorgeous tonight?' he said, still smiling at her. 'Now...' He turned back towards the others. 'Perhaps I'd better properly introduce myself while Audrey pops those flowers into water. Elliot Knight at your service. And you must be Mr Farnsworth, Audrey's father...'

Audrey spent the next couple of hours in a positive daze of delight. It was like a dream come true to have Elliot dancing attendance on her every whim, never leaving her side, insisting on sitting next to her at the table and generally playing the smitten lover better than she could have fantasised herself.

Despite knowing it was all an act, Audrey revelled in every single moment. She even felt herself blossoming under his attention, her usual tongue-tied reticence giving way to occasional bursts of witty conversation that had the other men giving her surprised but admiring glances.

It was during dessert that Audrey's joy in the evening became in danger of being dashed. A spectacular Bombe Alaska had just been brought to the table and Frances Liston laughingly made some comment about it reminding her of the ski slopes. Almost immediately, Lavinia looked across the expansive dining table straight at Elliot. 'Audrey mentioned you were down the slopes last weekend, Elliot. What resort did you stay at? Guthega? Thredbo? Perisher Valley?'

Audrey wished she could come up with some clever covering remark but fear of her charade being exposed brought an instant and speechless panic. Thankfully, Elliot was an intuitive and intelligent man. And not given to blank silences, although he did throw Audrey a drily amused smile before saying, 'None of them. I own a chalet overlooking Jindabyne Lake, which puts me within easy driving of all the nearby snowfields.'

Audrey's father looked impressed. Lavinia merely raised her eyebrows.

Edward, however, was never one to let tact override his curiosity. 'You must have a good job if you can own a chalet near the snowfields. What exactly do you do for a crust? Or shouldn't I ask?' he laughed.

Audrey cringed.

'I'm a corporate lawyer,' Elliot admitted graciously. 'I used to work for a large international company, but I recently came into a sizeable inheritance so I'm on unofficial long-service leave. I dare say when boredom sets in I'll return to active employment. Meanwhile...'

'Meanwhile?' Lavinia probed, not so graciously.

Audrey was fascinated, not only by this new information about Elliot, but at the way his mouth was pulling back into an incredibly charming and sensual smile. 'Meanwhile,' he said, turning slowly to bestow that smile on her own startled self, 'I have found other, far more interesting things to occupy my time.'

Colour flooded into Audrey's cheeks. No one sitting at that table could possibly misunderstand what he meant. Embarrassment warred with a crazy pleasure. Make-believe it all might be. But even a make-believe love-affair with Elliot was exciting.

'I must say I envy you,' Dwight remarked wryly. Which brought a sharp look from his wife. 'Not having to work, I mean,' he added awkwardly.

'Come now, Dwight,' Warwick Farnsworth chuckled expansively, 'you love your work. You'd go potty if you didn't spend ten hours every day behind that shiny desk of yours thinking up ways to market our products.'

'If all of you don't stop talking about work and eat your dessert,' Lavinia snapped, 'it will melt.'

They all fell to doing the dessert justice, Audrey welcoming the coolness of the ice-cream slipping down her throat. She was feeling very warm after Elliot's pointed remark. Very, very warm.

She couldn't help feeling pleased, however, that no one had looked surprised at Elliot's implication that they were lovers. Not even her father. She knew the reason too. Her improved appearance. Amazing how a woman's looks could change the way people thought of her, especially men. For a split second it struck her that maybe Elliot's attentions tonight were not all put on.

But only for a split second. Even as improved as her looks were, she still fell far short of the sort of female Elliot would go after.

Thinking about him sent her eyes sliding surreptitiously sidewards, her gaze settling on his classically handsome profile. It followed the lines of his strong straight nose down to his mouth, into which he was scooping the ice-cream with a steady rise and fall of his spoon.

Before she knew it Audrey was absorbed in watching him eat, watching his lips scoop the dessert into his mouth, definitely watching his tongue-tip whenever it darted out to capture any escaping droplets.

She couldn't take her eyes off him, couldn't stop thinking about what it might feel like to have those lips on hers again, to open her mouth beneath them, to have that tongue plunge forward.

A shivery but exquisite sensation rippled through her, bringing a small gasp of shock. *And* a slanted look from Elliot's cool grey eyes, which caught and locked on to hers.

His frown was instant and harsh, his expression troubled as his gaze searched for what lay behind her open-mouthed fascination. All too soon, he gave a slight head-shake, as well as a ragged sigh. Audrey snapped her head forwards and down, her insides curling with a shamed confusion at the knowingness in his eyes. What had he seen? What was he thinking?

She flinched when he leant over and whispered, 'No, Audrey. Definitely not.'

She blinked up at him, her cheeks burning with the fluster of the innocent. 'Definitely not what?'

His expression was rueful. 'Come now. You're not that naïve any more. Not after Russell. You must know now that little girls who play grown-up games sometimes get hurt.'

'I'm *not* a little girl,' she rasped, still not sure what he was referring to. She'd only been thinking about a kiss, after all.

Or had she?

'Precisely,' he agreed, an edge in his low voice. 'You're twenty-one years old and should know better than to start looking at frustrated males as if you want to eat them. Or is it the other way around?'

Wild, erotic visions burst into her mind with these words, making her reel with shock. How could this be herself thinking the sort of things she was thinking, wanting the sort of things she was wanting? She was shy where sex was concerned. Shy and inhibited and unadventurous.

At least, she *had* been. With Russell.

'I'm not going to become involved with you, Audrey,' Elliot muttered. 'Tonight's performance is a one-off thing. A favour. Now eat your dessert and stop making life difficult for the both of us.'

A cold wave of bitter reality washed through her, dousing her heated blood, obliterating her erotic fantasies. What in heaven's name was she doing, openly lusting after Elliot like that? Had she lost her senses? He'd made the facts perfectly clear the previous Friday. He found her too young, too in-experienced, too naïve, too vulnerable. Just be-cause she looked passably better tonight made no difference. He'd still only come to her party out of pity. How many times did she have to be reminded?

Audrey's humiliation was intense. Once again, she had made an utter fool of herself over a man. When would she ever learn?

The only safe harbour for her shame and her quickly withering self-respect was to do what she always did when situations became unbearable. She hibernated. Turned within herself, like a crab crawling into its shell. She would refuse to think. Or feel. And somehow, *somehow*, she would survive...

Meanwhile, the dinner party dragged on. Audrey's conversation died to no more than mono-syllabic replies, any smiles decidedly forced. If Elliot noticed her sudden lack of sparkle, he didn't say anything. But he seemed constrained too, as though he was regretting his decision to come.

Audrey could understand that. She was aching for the evening to end as much, if not more than he did.

Still, like the gentleman he was, Elliot remained doggedly by her side, even when they left the dining table and returned to the living-room where she dutifully cut the cake and opened her presents.

She'd just finished thanking her father for a lovely sapphire ring, the Hurleys for their French perfume and the Listons for a beautiful beaded evening purse when Lavinia announced coyly that Audrey's father had another special birthday sur-prise for his daughter.

Audrey was startled out of her semi-robotic state, her stepmother's expression enough to give her a prickling feeling of premonition. Lavinia looked like the cat who'd spotted the mouse and was zeroing in for the kill.

'Oh?' Audrey said warily. 'What?'

'You'll never guess,' Warwick Farnsworth said.

'Never in a million years,' Lavinia added in a silkily smug voice.

'You'll have to come outside to see it,' her father continued. 'Come on everyone. Come and see what I bought my Audrey for her coming of age.'

Audrey froze. Oh, my God, surely he wouldn't have. Surely not. Not a *car*! Not when he knew how she felt about driving. Surely he couldn't be that insensitive.

Elliot's taking of her arm gave her a jolt. She looked up into strong grey eyes, eyes that seemed to be saying, Don't worry. I'm here. But she was too stricken to take much comfort from them. For the first time that night, her mind was not on Elliot. It was rocketing back in time and hearing the squealing of brakes...the crunching of metal...her own screams.

She was only dimly aware of Elliot giving her chilled flesh a reassuring squeeze and leading her in her father's footsteps from the living-room to the main foyer, out through the front door and on to the patio.

And there it was. At the foot of those unending steps.

A car. A bright red Magna sedan.

She simply stared at it.

'Your father had it delivered while we were eating,' Lavinia said smarmily. 'I'll bet you're surprised, Audrey.'

Audrey said nothing. She was battling to control her feelings of appalled horror. How could he do this if he loved her, even a little? How *could* he?

'I know you always said you never wanted to drive, Audrey,' her father blustered when he encountered her deathly silence. 'But Lavinia and I discussed it and we decided it's over nine years since the accident and high time for you to put it behind you. Not driving won't bring your mother back, you know. One must conquer irrational fears, not give in to them, isn't that right, Lavinia?'

Lavinia smiled her agreement. 'Quite right, darling.'

Audrey felt panic closing in on her and without thinking she looked up at Elliot with plea-filled, stricken eyes.

His hesitation was only brief before he slid an arm round her waist and pulled her close to his side. 'Audrey's speechless with delight, aren't you, darling?' he drawled. 'And you're quite right, Warwick. An independent modern-day girl should know how to drive, and I see the Magna is an automatic. A piece of cake, Audrey. I'll teach you myself, if you like.'

Her voice only just worked as she blinked up at him. 'You would?' Impossible to keep the pained confusion out of her voice.

Elliot gave her a gently reassuring smile. 'Who else? We'll start tomorrow. Now, shouldn't you be thanking your father for such a marvellous gift? And your stepmama. I'm sure she had a hand in this.'

Was Audrey going mad or did she detect a heavy ironic tone in this last remark of Elliot's? Was he implying that the car had all been Lavinia's idea? That its choice had carried some malicious intent?

She looked with searching eyes over at her stepmother. The woman's mouth was smiling but the returning gaze was cold. Audrey's initial astonishment slowly changed to a seething, defiant anger.

I'll show her, she resolved bitterly. Her *and* my father. I'll learn to drive. I'll be the best damned driver this side of the Harbour Bridge! And when I am, I'm going to drive right out of their rotten selfish lives!

'It's a lovely car,' she said through clenched teeth. 'Thank you very much, Father...Lavinia... It's exactly what I wanted.'

Her father's huge smile of relief was so warm, so genuine, that Audrey was staggered. Maybe he *does* care, she realised, the knowledge stunning her. When he came forward to give her a big bear-hug, she was deeply moved. He does, she thought. He really does!

'I'm so glad, my dear,' he said as he pulled back. 'And somewhat relieved. To be truthful, I was rather worried about the car. But Lavinia was right, as usual. I have to congratulate you, darling.' He turned to hold out a hand to his wife. Lavinia took it, her smile looking as though it was cast in cement.

'Well, back inside, everyone,' Warwick boomed. 'It's too cold to stand around out here. Let's go and break out the port.'

Audrey and Elliot were the last inside, Audrey turning to Elliot after she'd shut the front door behind them. 'I seem to be always thanking you,' she said calmly enough, her discovery about her stepmother having given her an odd kind of strength. And determination. 'But thank you again.'

'You might not thank me tomorrow,' he said drily. 'They say men should never teach their girl-friends how to drive.'

Audrey was taken aback. 'But I'm not——'

Any further comment was terminated when he bent forward and kissed her lightly on the mouth. 'Big ears are listening,' he whispered against her lips. 'You don't want darling Lavinia to catch on, do you?' Then more loudly, 'Come on, Audrey. I haven't given you *my* present yet. Did you think you were only getting those flowers?'

Audrey was still reeling from Elliot's kiss when this other blow was delivered. She was simply beyond protest when he took her elbow and ushered her back into the living room with the others, drawing a slender velvet box from his jacket pocket as they went. He flipped it open and pressed it into her astonished hands.

She stared down at the exquisite gold necklace, her heart turning over. This was no cheap gift. This was worth hundreds of dollars. Audrey glanced up at Elliot in utter bewilderment.

'That's why I asked you not to wear any jewellery except gold earrings,' he explained lazily. 'So that I could do this...' And he took the heavy linked necklace from its velvet bed, turning her round to place it around her neck.

Goose-bumps flared all over her skin when she felt his fingertips feather against her bare flesh. She squeezed her eyes shut and tried hard to control her imagination, not to let it start wondering what it would be like to have those fingers all over her body.

She failed abysmally.

Her eyes finally fluttered back open, her cheeks pink, her heart thudding. Irritation at her continued stupidity fuelled a host of hot, angry thoughts. She would have to stop this futile fantasising over Elliot! Didn't she know there wasn't anything she could say or do to really interest a man like him? What was it he had said he'd been? A corporate lawyer? Well, handsome corporate lawyers didn't go for girls like her, even when they looked as presentable as they could and had just inherited a million or two. They bedded exciting, sensual, breathtakingly experienced women. Women like...

Against her will, her eyes were drawn to Lavinia.

Somehow Audrey already knew her stepmother wouldn't be looking at the gold necklace as everyone else was. Her coal-black gaze was fastened on Elliot and there was envy written all over her face. Not of the necklace, Audrey realised with a sick pang in her stomach, but of the giver.

# CHAPTER FOUR

AUDREY'S head automatically snapped up and around to see if Elliot was aware of Lavinia's lustful gaze. His eyes jerked away from something—or someone—to meet her searching glance with the remnants of a frown. For a second he stared at her, unseeing, before his face cleared. 'Don't you like my present?' he asked, nodding down at the gold necklace.

Any answer was thwarted by her father slapping Elliot on the shoulder. 'Of course she likes it! But beware, my man. Start giving a woman jewellery and she'll have you at the altar before you know it.'

'Oh, *Father*,' Audrey reproached, blushing with embarrassment.

'Yes, don't be ridiculous, Warwick,' Lavinia joined in waspishly. 'They've only just met. Besides, I can't see a man like Elliot giving up his bachelor status too easily.'

'Really, Lavinia?' Elliot's voice sounded reassuringly cool as he turned towards her. 'Then you'll be surprised to know I've already been married once. Didn't Audrey tell you? I'm a widower.'

The silence was quite electric for a moment before Elliot went on to quietly tell the surprised gathering the story behind his wife's tragic death. This brought a flurry of sympathetic murmurs, as well as some more questions, which revealed that the late Mrs Knight had been the famous children's

61

author, M. C. Thwaites, a piece of news that floored Audrey. She had seen M. C. Thwaites interviewed on television a couple of years back when one of her books had been awarded some special prize. Not only had the lady been very ordinary-looking, she had to have been at least ten years older than Elliot.

'But wasn't she around forty when she died?' Alice remarked, echoing Audrey's astonishment.

'Yes,' Elliot agreed. 'Moira was a few years older than me.'

'More than a few, surely,' Edward put in, as tactless as ever. 'You can't be much more than thirty.'

'Thirty-three, actually.'

Audrey tried not to show her shock. But her mind was reeling. She'd envisaged Moira as a stunning, exquisitely feminine creature whom Elliot had loved to distraction. A woman like Lavinia. Audrey just couldn't picture him madly in love with the un-doubtedly clever but rather homely author.

Ugly suspicions leapt into Audrey's mind, only to be shakily dismissed. *Her* Elliot wouldn't do such a thing as marry a rich older sick woman simply for her money. He *wouldn't*! Besides, he'd said he loved his wife. *Hadn't* he? Or had he just denied marrying the lady for her money? She couldn't remember . . .

Some rhythmic music was put on and Audrey dimly heard Lavinia's voice urging everyone to dance. 'Stop frowning, birthday girl,' Elliot murmured into her ear, 'and dance with me. It's expected of us.'

'What?' She glanced up into Elliot's openly handsome face and felt instantly guilty at doubting this man who'd been so kind to her; was *still* being kind. 'All right,' she smiled gratefully, 'but I'm not a very good dancer.'

'Don't worry. I'm no Fred Astaire myself.' But he drew her quite confidently into his arms, steering her smoothly across the carpet and out into the foyer where the slate floor made an excellent dance-floor.

Audrey did her utmost to dance as well as her limited experience could manage, but the feel of Elliot's lean hard body pressed against her did little for her composure, and when she finally tripped over his toes her dismay was acute. 'S . . . sorry,' she stammered. 'I'm a clumsy clot.'

'Don't be silly,' he returned, and drew her back into his arms, pressing her even closer. But he stopped moving her around the floor quite so much, reducing their movements to a gentle swaying and the odd twirl. Soon Audrey was so enveloped in the sensual warmth of his embrace that she totally relaxed, closing her eyes and nestling her head under Elliot's chin, enjoying the moment for what it was. She was under no illusions that this was where Elliot would normally choose to be—in *her* arms—but she refused to think like that tonight. Tonight he was hers. If *he* could pretend so well then so could she.

Suddenly, the music was snapped off.

Audrey's eyes fluttered open to look over her shoulder and see Lavinia at the CD player, glaring coldly over at her before swinging a gay smile round to the others. 'Warwick's just opened the port, everyone. And there's coffee here for those who would prefer it.'

Audrey heard Elliot mutter a word under his breath that sounded suspiciously like 'bitch'. But she couldn't be sure. When he drew back from their embrace, his expression was implacably cool. 'Coffee, my lady?' he suggested with a gallant little bow and an outstretched hand.

Audrey laughed, and took his hand. But any real pleasure in the rest of the evening and Elliot's company was spoiled by her stepmother's continuing looks. Sour to her; seductive to Elliot. Audrey was on tenterhooks, wondering what Lavinia would say or do next. Once, the woman sat down next to him and actually put her hand oh, so casually on his thigh. Elliot didn't bat an eyelash. Audrey wanted to tear her stepmother's eyes out.

In a way, she was glad when the party broke up shortly after midnight and the guests started to go home, despite her not wanting Elliot to leave.

He lingered behind, however, and Audrey's father jumped to the conclusion that he wanted some time alone with Audrey, announcing with a nod and a wink that Lavinia and he would retire upstairs and 'leave the young ones to it'. Lavinia looked livid at this remark, retorting with sweet sarcasm that she was hardly old at thirty-seven. Warwick totally ignored her, took her elbow and ushered her firmly from the room.

Audrey expelled a quavering breath once they were gone. 'I'm so sorry, Elliot,' she murmured.

They were sitting on the same sofa, sipping the remains of a last cup of coffee, a fair distance between them. Elliot gave her an unreadable glance.

'Sorry for what?'

'For putting you through this charade. For your having to answer all those questions. And for Lavinia.'

'Ah, yes...Lavinia... She was rather obvious, wasn't she?'

Her stomach contracted. 'Yes,' she admitted unhappily.

'Let's hope your father didn't notice.'

Audrey looked at him as he swallowed the last of his coffee and put down the cup. There was no doubt he was a striking man, in every way. His looks, his style, his air of contained self-confidence. He wasn't even unduly bothered by being treated like a sex object. 'Does...does this sort of thing happen to you often?' she asked hesitantly.

Elliot shrugged. 'Let's just say it happens more than I'd like.'

'Doesn't it get boring?' she said sharply, her jealousy emerging again.

'Yes,' he agreed with a distaste she found quite reassuring, till she remembered she herself had been guilty of similar behaviour at the dinner table. A shameful blush crept into her cheeks. She hated to think that Elliot was lumping her in the same category as Lavinia. It wasn't just lust she felt. She loved the man. She'd been sure the moment she opened the door tonight. So sure she had almost cried.

A heavy silence fell between them, almost as heavy as Audrey's heart.

Suddenly, Elliot got to his feet, forcing her to look up at him.

'I must be going,' he said matter-of-factly. 'I need eight hours' sleep if I'm to be a bright and breezy driving instructor in the morning.'

Her chest tightened. She had forgotten about the car. And the driving lessons. Oh, God... She didn't know which would be worse, trying to conquer her

fear of driving, or continuing to see Elliot. Both
would bring her pain, one from the past, the other
ongoing.

Audrey closed her eyes for a moment, then
opened them and stood up. 'You ... you don't have
to, you know,' she said in a strangled voice, her
eyes bleak. 'I could always go to a driving school.'

'Is that what you'd prefer to do?' he asked softly.

She did her best to keep her gaze steady, to hide
the emotions she felt sure had to be mirrored in
them. The love ... the need ... the yearning ...

At the final moment she couldn't lie. 'No,' she
confessed. 'I'd rather you teach me.'

He said absolutely nothing, frowning grey eyes
skating over her as she stood there. She felt
awkward and far too aware of him.

'I ... I know you don't really want to,' she went
on shakily. 'You're just being kind again.'

The muscles in his jaw flinched. 'Is there some
crime against being kind?'

'No ... But no one likes to be pitied!' she added
with a flash of fire.

His sigh was frustrated. 'Who said what I feel
for you is pity?'

'Oh, do be honest, Elliot,' she flared some more.
'Do you think I don't know why you came tonight,
why you covered up for me, why you even gave me
this beautiful necklace?' She touched it with
tremulous fingers.

He reached out to curl strong hands over her
shoulders, his expression almost angry. 'You don't
know the first damned thing about why I came here
tonight,' he ground out. 'You don't know anything
about me at all except what you've been romanti-
cising in that idealistic young head of yours. I'm

not a kind man, Audrey. Not at all. But I *am* honest. Sure, I pitied you. Why not? You've had a rough deal from what I can see. You needed someone on your side for once and I elected myself. But if you think I'm the original White Knight you couldn't be more mistaken. I can be as black as the next bastard. Blacker even than your Russell!'

He gave a bitter laugh. 'Want some more honesty? Well, you're perfectly correct. I *don't* want to teach you to drive. I don't want to see you again at all. But it's not because of the reasons your inferiority complex is sure to invent. Quite the opposite, in fact. It's because I'm worried I might end up seducing you, you silly little fool.'

Audrey blinked up at him in amazement. What was he saying? That he found her attractive, even *desirable*? The idea sent her heart thudding madly in her chest.

'Even now I have this crazy impulse to kiss you,' he raved on, his grip tightening on her shoulders. 'The trouble is I won't want to stop with kissing. Before I know it, I'll want soft flesh under my hands. Soft...warm...moist...female...flesh. I'll want to sink into that flesh, lose myself in it. Touch it...taste it...'

Audrey's whole head was positively whirling. She could do nothing but stand there, staring up at him in breathless arousal, his evocatively explicit words blasting hot images into her brain, sending the blood roaring through her veins.

For a long long moment he glared down at her, grey eyes glittering. And then his head began moving, sinking down towards her, his impassioned gaze intent on her mouth.

Her lips parted in a silent gasp.

He's going to kiss me, she thought in a dazed wonder.

But then he suddenly straightened, a deep shudder reverberating through him as he reefed his hands away from her body and stepped backward.

'Dammit,' he growled. 'I can't. I *mustn't*!'

'But...but why not?' she burst out in a surge of compulsive desire. 'I...I want you to kiss me. I want you to make love to me,' she finished, every part of her starting to quiver.

He was tempted. She could see he was tempted. His eyes locked on to her mouth, his whole body filled with a vibrating tension that brought an electric atmosphere to the room. Audrey scooped in and held her breath, hardly daring to imagine what was coming next. She still hadn't come to terms with what she herself had just said. My God, she had never been so bold in her whole life!

But at the last second he groaned and whirled away, his hands literally shaking as they raked back through his thick dark hair. He uttered an obscenity under his breath, then strode over to pour himself a drink from one of the decanters resting next to the remains of her birthday cake. It looked like bourbon.

Audrey watched with her mouth open as he downed the whisky with one swallow. What was he going to do? she wondered in breathless excitement. But when he swung back to face her, eyes full of a furious exasperation, she took a nervous step backwards.

'Haven't you learnt anything at all from your experience with Russell?' he flung across the room at her. 'For God's sake, Audrey, you don't go offering yourself like that to men you don't really know.'

'But I...I do know you,' she protested in confusion.

'What do you know?' he scoffed. 'My age? My marital status? My qualifications? What do they tell you about what sort of man I really am...inside? Not a damned thing!'

'I know that you're good and kind,' she insisted. 'I know you wouldn't deliberately hurt me.'

His laughter was bitter. 'You haven't listened to a word I've said, have you?' He began to walk slowly back towards her, his expression sardonic. 'I'm none of those things. I'm merely suffering from a lingering conscience after living with a woman like Moira. Some of her character must have rubbed off on me. But I doubt it will last. Fact is,' he drawled, his eyes dropping to where her breasts were rising and falling beneath the tight cream silk, 'I can feel it weakening already.'

Her face flamed as her nipples sprang to attention under his smouldering gaze.

'Good and kind,' he scorned. And with a stunning swiftness grabbed her, yanking her hard against him, enfolding her trembling softness within a body which, at that moment, was totally terrifyingly hard. 'Good and kind!' he repeated, laughing, both hands sliding up to hold the back of her head in a vice-like grip. 'Would a good and kind man do this?'

His mouth was hot and angry as it closed over hers. Totally without compromise. Totally without conscience. It demanded and took, brooking no opposition, no struggles this time. It forced her lips apart, forced her to accept his thrusting tongue with an aggressive dominance that took her breath away.

It was not the sort of kiss Audrey had dreamt about from Elliot. Not at all. But much as a part of her was shocked—even frightened—by the quality of violence in his actions, her feelings for this man would not allow her to remain unmoved under such a passionate onslaught. Within seconds she was responding, her own desire sparking a speedy willingness, her lips falling further open beneath his. Her arms tore out from where they'd been squashed between them, wrapping themselves securely around his hard male torso.

His mouth gasped from hers, as though in shock of such co-operation. But it quickly returned, more gently this time, giving Audrey a glimpse of true sexual expertise. Now Elliot *was* seducing her, his tongue playing with hers, his hands cradling her head. His thumbs started rubbing tantalisingly over her ears, her lobes, making her shiver with delight. He kept turning her head this way and that, exploring different sections of her mouth, each foray of his tongue sending shuddering waves of heat and excitement all through her.

It became harder to think. Harder and harder. All she knew was that it hadn't been like this with Russell. Not even remotely.

When a dazed moan came from deep within her throat, Elliot actually trembled, groaning and gathering her even tighter against him. One hand remained to splay up into her hair, the other sweeping down her spine, then over the swell of her buttocks. She could feel the heat of his hand through her dress as it moulded over one of her cheeks, squeezing it, grasping it, lifting and pressing her body hard against his. She could feel his arousal against her.

Once again, his mouth tore away from hers, this time to traverse down her throat, leaving a moist, ravaged trail behind. She gasped, then groaned when he started sucking her flesh, tipping her head back in a gesture of sheer ecstasy. She gasped even more when he swept her up into his arms and began to carry her from the room.

'Where's your room?' he rasped, already striding across the foyer and heading for the stairs.

'The first...first on the r...right,' she stammered, momentarily stunned by the speed with which everything was happening.

It was as he began taking the steps two at a time that she remembered the one impediment to what he was obviously intending to do.

'Elliot,' she choked out. 'We *can't*!'

Clearly the desperate anguish in her voice communicated itself to him for he faltered, glaring down at her with eyes she barely recognised. There was none of the cool sophisticate in those turbulent grey pools at that moment. 'What do you mean, we *can't*?' he growled. 'What's to stop us?'

'Me. I mean, I...I have my period,' she said in a small voice.

'Your period,' he repeated flatly, and closed his eyes.

'I'm sorry,' she whispered, feeling deeply embarrassed and physically wretched. Did he think she didn't want him too? My God, she ached from wanting him.

'She's sorry...' He shook his head and opened his eyes. They looked terrible. 'God,' he exhaled, and lowered her on to the first landing. He turned and gripped the balustrade, breathing deeply several times. Finally, he heaved one last shuddering sigh then turned, soothing her anxiety with a sincerely apologetic look. '*I'm* the one who should be saying sorry. Hell, I don't know what got into me. I didn't even think of contraception. Believe me, Audrey, when I say that Mother Nature has just saved you from making the biggest mistake in your life!'

She stared over at him, her heart breaking. She didn't see it that way at all. Oh, she knew he didn't love her and probably never would. But she couldn't change that, just as she couldn't change the way she felt about him. She loved him—quite madly— and would have treasured the experience of having him make love to her. Maybe nothing more permanent would have come of it, but she would at least have had one time with him.

But no...fate wasn't going to allow her even that small concession to happiness.

She could have cried when he cupped her face with warm, tender hands. 'It's all for the best,' he said gently. 'It's love you should be looking for, Audrey. Not sex. And the truth is, I'm flush out of love at the moment. To give a young vulnerable girl like you one without the other would be criminal, especially so soon after Russell.'

Audrey went to splutter something, something about how she didn't give a fig for Russell, but he silenced her with a look.

'If you think this is easy for me,' he went on grimly, 'you're mistaken. The easy course would be to take you and use you, then tell you one day that your services would be no longer required, that I was moving on to someone else. Believe me, I'm well acquainted with the sort of man who could do that. I was one for twenty-nine years and could well be again. Commitment does not come naturally to me.'

Audrey blinked up at him, shocked. What was he saying? That before his marriage he had been an incurable Don Juan, a callous Casanova? Much as he had the sort of looks and sex appeal that could lead to a man becoming a womaniser, she couldn't believe he was. A hardened rake would have responded to Lavinia's sexual overtures. He also certainly wouldn't be caring about a young girl's emotional and physical welfare. Perhaps he might have been a cad once, but he wasn't any longer. It was a case of actions speaking more loudly than words.

'Are you listening to me, Audrey?' he demanded in an impatient tone.

'I—er—yes.'

'You don't seem to be. Let me put it into simple terms. I'm not going to sleep with you. I'll be your friend, if you still want me to be. You don't seem to have many of those. But for pity's sake, *don't* go complicating things by falling in love with me. It would only be a rebound thing anyway, after Russell. Give yourself time to find your feet before you launch into another romance. Another man will come along eventually, a man of your own age who'll truly love you and won't hurt you. Meanwhile . . .'

Her heart leapt. 'Meanwhile?'

His mouth curved back into a cynical twist. 'Meanwhile, I'll have to make sure I don't go jumping on you during your driving lessons. You seem to be a sensual sort of girl, very easy to turn on. Why Russell called you a bore in bed I have no idea! Perhaps I'll have to take up jogging...or maybe...'

His eyes clouded with thought.

Audrey's stomach turned over when she realised he was contemplating taking a lover, some experienced woman who would meet his sexual needs and so turn him into a 'safe' friend for her.

Desolation ripped through her. You don't have to do that, she wanted to scream at him. I'm not that young or naïve or vulnerable any more. I know the score. I know it's just sex you want. I understand. Truly I do. But I won't demand anything. All I want is to lie with you and comfort you. Don't waste my love. Don't let it wither and die, unenjoyed, untried, unfulfilled...

She stared up into his handsome face, the words bursting from her heart. But she said nothing, her desolate sigh snapping Elliot out of his reverie. 'You'd better get to bed, Audrey,' he said. 'You look tired.'

She nodded resignedly, hating herself for her silence, even though logic told her any offer she made to be Elliot's mistress would be a waste of time. He wouldn't say yes. She tried telling herself this was because he was protecting her from further hurt, but a familiar old voice kept whispering that if she were really beautiful and sexy, he wouldn't be able to turn her down so easily.

'Don't bother seeing me out,' he was saying. 'I know the way. Will ten be too early for you in the morning?'

'Could...could you make it eleven?' She had a feeling it would take her a long time to get to sleep tonight, regardless of how tired she was.

'Eleven, then.' He stepped forward and gave her a very platonic peck on the forehead. 'Goodnight, Birthday Girl.'

Audrey watched him leave, her heart sinking as far as it could go.

'Oh, Elliot,' she sighed, then turned and trudged up to bed.

She was right; it took her a very long time to get to sleep.

# CHAPTER FIVE

'YOU certainly are a dark horse, Audrey, latching on to a man like that!'

Lavinia swept into the kitchen, a sensual vision in a purple velvet dressing-gown, her long black hair flowing out over her shoulders.

Audrey groaned silently, her eyes lifting from her coffee-cup to the wall clock to check she hadn't lost an hour or two. Her stepmother rarely rose on a Saturday before midday. But no, it was only ten forty-four. 'You're up early,' she said, ignoring the comment about Elliot.

Lavinia made a scoffing sound. 'I couldn't get back to sleep after Warwick made so much noise going to golf this morning. And now I've got a headache.' She busied herself finding some pain-killers in the medicine cabinet above the re-frigerator, washing them down with a glass of water.

Audrey remained perched on her stool at the breakfast bar, downing her coffee as fast as possible. After last night's eye-opening per-formance, she knew that Lavinia hadn't come down here just for some aspirin—there was an adequate supply in her bathroom—and, quite frankly, she wasn't in the mood for her stepmother's two-faced manoeuvrings.

But she wasn't quick enough. Before she could escape, Lavinia was on the other side of the counter, giving her an uncompromising stare. 'Well? Aren't you going to tell me all about the enigmatic Mr Knight?'

Audrey effected what she hoped was a nonchalant shrug. 'What's to tell? I thought Elliot told you everything about himself last night.'

'Hardly. He only gave us the bare facts. Truly, Audrey, what kind of game are you playing?'

'Game?' Audrey could feel a guilty blush coming into her cheeks. 'What do you mean?'

'Well, you must have known a man like that would come as a shock to your father and myself. Let's face it, he's hardly what we were expecting. We did our best to hide our feelings last night, but surely you can see the man's far too old for you, among other things.'

Audrey glared up at her stepmother, thinking that *she* hadn't hidden her feelings at all. Lavinia had lusted after Elliot like a bitch on heat. 'Oh?' Her voice was taut, her throat convulsing as she battled to keep her anger under control. 'I thought Father seemed to like Elliot. *You* certainly did.'

Lavinia looked momentarily rattled by this last pointed remark. But she recovered quickly. 'Well, of course we liked him. Mr Knight is an accomplished charmer. A *very* accomplished charmer. But one with a vague background, not to mention an odd marriage to a very wealthy older woman. One wonders how soon there would have been a divorce if his poor wife hadn't passed away so conveniently. I hear she was extremely plain.' Her hard black gaze flicked over Audrey in a dismissive fashion. 'It must have occurred to you that Elliot Knight is basically just another Russell.'

Audrey's heart squeezed tight as she fought to keep her breathing calm, her face composed.

'Another Russell? I'm afraid I don't see the simi-
larity at all.'

'Oh, you poor dear sweet naïve darling,' her
stepmother sighed. 'I thought you would have
realised. Russell was only after your money, you
know. Your father and I guessed that right from
the start.'

Audrey was having difficulty stopping her sim-
mering anger from taking over. Lavinia's tactics
were all too clear now. Deliver an undermining
insult within cleverly disguised endearments, then
sit back and revel in the damage done. Why she
had to do this Audrey couldn't guess. Some sort
of jealousy perhaps. Or sheer natural bitchiness.
She didn't know and didn't really care. She only
knew she wasn't going to be a willing victim any
longer.

Audrey put down the coffee-cup she'd been
clasping like a life-line. 'Is that so?' she bit out.
'Then why in heaven's name didn't you warn me?
What purpose could you and Father have for
leaving me in the dark?'

Astonishment at being openly confronted
widened those cold black eyes. 'Well, I—er—we
didn't want to hurt you, dear. Besides, Warwick
thought it would do you good to get out and about
a bit, regardless.'

'You mean to tell me that Father tolerated some
gigolo's seducing me with an eye to the family
fortune, in exchange for my having a few dates?
How amazing! I'll have to ask him to explain his
reasoning when he gets home. I would have thought
he'd be furious that he had such a creep in his
employ!'

'Well, of course Warwick didn't think Russell had actually *seduced* you, Audrey,' Lavinia blustered.

'Oh? You mean he believed a man like that would take me out continuously for a few months and not try anything. How flattering!' She affected a drily amused laugh.

Lavinia stared at her as though she didn't recognise her stepdaughter, or her new manner. 'No...he...I... Well, the fact is, my dear, I told Warwick he hadn't. Your father came to me expressing concern about you, so I thought it best to soothe his fears. I said that you had confided in me and told me Russell was being a perfect gentleman.'

Audrey's heart caught at the knowledge that her father had not been as guilty of negligence concerning her welfare as she had feared. It reaffirmed the hope that he did love her after all.

But her anger at Lavinia only increased. Oddly enough, it soothed her soul to keep that anger in check, to use its strengthening force to overcome her usual lack of assertion. 'But why would you do that, Lavinia?' she questioned relentlessly.

'I...I...' Her stepmother's fluster was evidenced in her stammering voice and the high colour in her face. 'I didn't want to worry Warwick,' she blurted out before pulling herself together, tossing her head in a prickly haughtiness. 'You know what fathers are like. They worry about things like that.'

Audrey was about to deny knowing any such thing when Lavinia smiled, a slow sly smile that made her skin crawl. 'But we women know we don't really mind being made love to by men like Russell,' she drawled. 'Wicked men can be very exciting, can't they? Men like Elliot——'

'Elliot's not wicked!' Audrey defended, her composure slipping for a second.

'Isn't he?' Lavinia laughed again, only this time, it had a smug tone to it. 'Quite clearly you don't really know the man. You certainly haven't been to bed with him as yet or you wouldn't be making such a naïve statement.' She gave her stepdaughter a pitying glance. 'Let me give you a little tip, dear. Don't play too hard to get. You're not *that* rich.'

And with this final *coup de grâce* she swept from the room.

Audrey sat there, shaking. The bitch! The miserable rotten jealous bitch!

She was still sitting there a few seconds later, trying to contain her rage and her pain, when the sounds of the grandfather clock bonging eleven drifted through the still swinging kitchen door. Almost simultaneously, the front doorbell rang.

'Oh, no...Elliot,' she groaned.

Rather a different reaction from that to his arrival last night, Audrey thought with a despairing bleakness as she levered herself off the stool and moved reluctantly towards the front door. If it weren't for Lavinia she would tell him she had changed her mind and would learn to drive elsewhere, thereby ending this friendship before it could cause her any more misery. But she just couldn't bear the thought of her stepmother gloating.

An idea, however, slipped into Audrey's mind as she reached for the doorknob, an idea that would eliminate the problem of Lavinia quite effectively. She wondered why she hadn't thought of it before.

But, once again, the sight of Elliot stunned her, throwing her mind off-track. Dressed in a navy blue tracksuit, white T-shirt and trainers, he looked even more sexy than he had the previous night. Perhaps it was his unshaven face that gave him such a raw appeal. Or his wind-blown hair, flopping over his forehead. Or maybe it was the looser, more casual clothes, drawing attention to the athletic power of his impressive male body, from his wide shoulders down to his lean hips and long muscular thighs.

She couldn't help remembering how it had felt last night with those thighs hard against hers.

'Good morning, Birthday Girl,' he greeted, grey eyes smiling. 'Nice day, isn't it? Sun shining. No wind. Sydney at its winter best. I've been up since seven, being a good little jogger. Hey...' He gave her a close look. 'You don't look so hot. Are you sure you want your first driving lesson today? I could come back tomorrow.'

Her mind snapped back to reality, though her heart still pounded away. God, there was no way she would be able to concentrate on learning to drive sitting next to Elliot in the close confines of a car. No way...

Yet to put him off, to turn round and re-enter that house and face Lavinia's smug questions, was unthinkable. The idea she'd had a moment ago, that of moving out of home and into a flat of her own, would take time to implement. But at least it would ensure that when Elliot disappeared from the scene—which he ultimately would—Lavinia wouldn't be around to make nasty cutting remarks.

Meanwhile, she would have to go with him and put up with his trying to teach her to drive for a few days. Maybe she could look upon it as a trial for her new self, the one who had resolved overnight to take charge of her own life from this day forward.

'No,' she said tautly. 'No point in putting off the unpleasant.'

'Is that how you think of me?' Elliot laughed. 'As unpleasant?'

She thought she did splendidly, keeping her expression calm. 'Not you, Elliot. Learning to drive. I must warn you, though. I might prove unteachable.'

'Never! You're a very quick learner.' His eyes flicked over her face and hair with definite satisfaction before dropping to admire her plain peach-coloured shirt. 'Not only have you very sensibly kept your hair up and your make-up neutral, but you've also discovered that more subdued colours suit you much better than brighter ones.'

Audrey felt herself pinkening with pleasure. She had gone through her wardrobe this morning, tossing aside everything that hit her in the eye. Which hadn't left her much to choose from. She'd come up with the plain shirt Elliot had just admired and her favourite stone-washed grey jeans, jeans which Elliot was now staring at with a definite frown.

'Those jeans, though,' he added with a wry grimace. 'I suggest you leave them in your wardrobe in future when you go out with me.'

Now Audrey was taken aback. And quite put out. 'Those jeans' were the one item of clothing she'd never doubted looked good on her. If she'd been able to wear them everywhere, she would have.

'What's wrong with them?' she demanded to know quite crossly. 'Surely you're not one of those old-fashioned men who like women in dresses and skirts all the time? I happen to like these jeans and

I intend wearing them whenever and wherever I want to!'

Now it was Elliot's turn to be taken aback, whether because of her accusing him of being old-fashioned or her standing up for herself Audrey wasn't sure. But she was fed up with being confused by people telling her what to wear and what not to wear. Perhaps it was her own stupid fault, never having had a mind of her own. But that was going to be a thing of the past. In future she would definitely make her own decisions, in every facet of her life. And if she made mistakes, then tough! At least they would be *her* mistakes.

'What's got into *you* this morning?'

'Nothing,' she grumped, then sighed. 'I'm sorry, Elliot. I guess I'm in a bit of a cantakerous mood.'

'No, don't apologise. It's great. I love it. It's just such a surprise to find that sweet shy Audrey has found some real spit and fire. Not to mention the courage of her own convictions for once.'

'Well, that's a backhanded compliment, if ever there was one!' she huffed.

'God! There's more of it! Next thing the claws will come out and I'll be ducking for cover.'

When she tried to glare at him, she was totally disarmed by his infectious grin. 'You're a meanie,' she accused, though smiling.

'Never!'

'*And* a bad judge of clothes. These jeans look good on me.'

'Yes,' he agreed, jaw clenching as his eyes dropped once again to where the stretch denim hugged every curve of her shapely legs and bottom. 'That's the problem.'

His gaze travelled back up, lingering over the thrust of her breasts under the cotton shirt. When his eyes finally lifted to lock with hers, her breath caught in her throat. Elliot wasn't making any attempt to hide his desire-filled state.

He really wants me, she thought, thunder-struck.

His frown was swift and dark as the same thought apparently struck him.

The charged moment was interrupted by the front door being yanked fully open behind them.

'Audrey! Why are you standing out here with the front door half open? It's creating a draught and it's... Oh, it's you, Elliot,' Lavinia gushed, pretending to be totally surprised by his presence as she came out on to the front porch. One red-nailed hand clutched her velvet dressing-gown inadequately shut over an obviously naked bosom, the other brushing her long black waves back from her face with primping movements. 'I didn't realise you were here. I've just got up out of bed.'

Audrey scrutinised her stepmother's fully made-up face with newly cynical eyes. She also didn't miss the exotic perfume wafting from the woman in intoxicating waves. Any other female would know exactly what Lavinia was up to. Audrey hoped Elliot was equally *au fait* with such blatant womanly wiles.

Jealousy twisted inside her when she noticed his eyes transfixed on her stepmother's cleavage, those eyes which a second before had been gleaming at *her* with undisguised desire. So much for her thinking he wanted her exclusively. He probably looked at a lot of women like that!

Her glare must have attracted his attention for his eyes slid her way, his expression quickly projecting a measure of exasperation with her. But not a trace of guilt.

Lavinia's words came back to haunt her, about Elliot's being wicked, something she would know if he'd made love to her. Clearly her stepmother had meant sexually wicked. But did that mean he would be an adventurous lover? Imaginative? Inventive? Or that sex for him was a vice, a hedonistic pleasure separated from all caring and feeling, to be indulged in indiscriminately, without morals and conscience.

Despite what had just happened, Audrey rejected such a concept quite fiercely. No! That couldn't be so. If that was so he would never have been such a gentleman with her, neither the first day they met nor last night. Certainly not last night when he had been so aroused. A wicked man would have bent her to his will anyway, found some alternative way to satisfy his lust.

Though relatively inexperienced, Audrey was not a total ignoramus where sex was concerned. Russell himself had suggested such...alternatives...to her on occasions, but she had been repulsed and had refused. Audrey had to admit that she might not be repulsed if Elliot made similar demands. She suspected she would be only too willing, a thought that brought her up with a jolt. Much as she loved Elliot and wanted to make love with him, she would never be prepared to be callously used, to be treated like a whore!

The word whore sent her gaze back to Lavinia, who was continuing to flirt outrageously with Elliot. 'You must come to dinner one night, when there are no other guests. We'd love to have you.'

You mean *you'd* love to have him, Audrey thought with a mixture of savage anger and out-right panic. Dear God, please don't let that happen. Not that. Anything but that...

'Love to,' Elliot responded suavely. 'Give me a ring some time and we can co-ordinate dates. Now I must be getting on with teaching madam here to drive. Have you got the keys to the Magna, Audrey?'

'They're just inside on the hall table.'

'Well, get them, sweet thing. I haven't got all day.'

'Going out later?' Audrey heard Lavinia ask as she hurried into the foyer.

'Not out,' came the reply. 'I want to listen to the races this afternoon.'

'Oh, you're a gambler!' Lavinia sounded de-lighted. 'I love people who gamble. They're so daring.'

Elliot gave a dry laugh. 'Really? I'd call them stupid. No, I'm not a gambler. I inherited a share in a racehorse and since I don't like to be ignorant I'm doing a crash course in punting before I attend her first race next Saturday.'

Audrey rejoined Elliot where he'd moved down a step or two, away from Lavinia.

'How exciting!' she was saying. 'Where *are* the races next Saturday?'

'Rosehill. I'm taking Audrey,' he said, and hooked an arm through her elbow.

Luckily, Audrey was getting rather used to Elliot's ingenuity and didn't register any betraying surprise. 'Yes,' she agreed. 'I can't wait.'

'Sorry I can't invite you and Warwick to come along too, Lavinia,' Elliot went on. 'But we're going to be the guests of some friends of mine in their private box. Maybe another time...'

'Yes, of course,' Lavinia excused with a stiff smile, but Audrey saw the flash of pique in her eyes. She thanked God Elliot had wangled his way out of that one.

'Come along, Audrey...' Elliot made a point of guiding her with extra care down the steep steps as though she was some fragile flower that needed gentle handling.

She threw him a slightly sarcastic look once they reached bottom. 'Don't you think you're over-doing it a bit?'

'Perhaps,' he agreed, grinning.

Truly! He was really enjoying himself, playing out this charade. It crossed her mind that Elliot could be right about her not knowing his motives in helping her. Perhaps it wasn't out of kindness, or pity. Perhaps he was getting a kick out of acting the part of gallant lover. Perhaps he simply enjoyed deception.

Or perhaps there was some other devious reason she hadn't yet thought of...

An uneasy feeling crept over her as she watched him open the passenger door for her, a rather wry smile on his face. He'd said she didn't really know anything about him and this was becoming more evident every time they met. A *racehorse* now, for heaven's sake! What next?

'Audrey? Hop in.'

She blinked. 'Where...where are you taking me?' she asked with a twinge of unexpected alarm.

'Somewhere very isolated where we won't meet any other cars.'

'Isolated?' she repeated, swallowing.

'That's right. You haven't got your learner's licence or your L plates yet, and we can't get them this morning. The Motor Registry Office is closed on a Saturday. That means we'll have to keep well off the main roads. Still, you won't be ready for traffic for a while yet, anyway. Come on. Get in. Can't have you having an accident,' he whispered to her as she brushed past him to climb into the car. 'The wicked witch would probably like that.'

Audrey's eyes snapped round and up, widening with shock. She glanced agitatedly over Elliot's shoulder up at the house, but Lavinia had already gone inside.

'OK, so she probably doesn't want you dead,' Elliot drawled. 'But a little mangled she wouldn't mind.' He shut the car door with a bang.

It was a full five minutes before Audrey could speak a word. By then Elliot was behind the wheel of the Magna and well on his way to finding an 'isolated' place. Audrey's thoughts, however, were no longer on Elliot or his motives or even her imminent driving lessons. It was concentrated on the woman who had influenced her life over the past nine years, influenced it not to Audrey's advantage. Lavinia had picked away at her confidence, undermined her self-esteem, made her feel insecure in her father's love. Now Elliot seemed to think she might actually wish her physical harm.

'I don't understand any of this,' she said agitatedly. 'Why does she hate me so?'

'Women like Lavinia don't hate,' Elliot pronounced bluntly. 'That would presuppose a capacity to love. They compete. With every other female that comes within their circle. They want— no, *need*—to be the centre of attention. They mistakenly think this solely relies on their looks. Lavinia would see any woman as a potential threat, Audrey. You most of all.'

'But...but that doesn't make sense!' Audrey blurted out. 'How could I ever compete with Lavinia's looks? I mean...I'll never be as beautiful as she is.'

'Oh, I wouldn't say that. You looked pretty good to me last night. You're also young and fresh and innocent. They're things *she* can never be again. Besides, there are many types of beauty, Audrey. Admittedly, Lavinia is a very striking woman, but rather flashy. Some men don't care for that type.'

'*You* seemed to back at the house,' she snapped before she could snatch it back.

Elliot slowed down at an amber light, darting her a sardonic look once the car actually stopped. 'I've been waiting for that, ever since you caught me staring at those eye-popping breasts of hers. Look, I'm a normal male, Audrey, with twenty-twenty vision. But, believe me, I can admire the way Mother Nature has put a woman together, without admiring the woman beneath. I'd much rather go to bed with you, my love, than the likes of your stepmother.'

Audrey's heart jumped, a discomfiting heat warming her cheeks. 'I wish you wouldn't say things like that,' she mumbled.

'Why?'

Annoyance at his insensitivity snapped her eyes his way. 'Because I...I...' She shook her head, unable to put the truth into words.

'Because you still want me to make love to you?' he asked quietly.

She froze.

'You may as well say it. Or I might think you haven't decided to take control of your own life after all.'

Her head turned slowly his way, their eyes meeting. She was astonished at how calm his were. But he was right. What was the point in promising herself to be different from now on if she never acted upon it?

'Yes,' she confessed, though it came out in a hoarse whisper.

His eyes flickered slightly. 'Yes what?'

'Yes, I still want you to make love to me.'

Her satisfaction was strong as the words came out, steady and sure.

He held her gaze for ages, the silence in the car deafening.

'I'm not sure if you're still a fool, Audrey Farnsworth,' he said at last, his voice low and almost angry, 'or the most devious young woman I've ever met.'

She gaped at him.

He sighed, his frustration obvious. 'God knows you confuse me more than any female I've ever met. I don't know if I want to kiss you, or take you over my knee and smack your very delectable bottom. Either way I'll probably still end up in bed with you, you cunning little minx.'

He made an exasperated sound. Audrey merely stared at him, enthralled and bemused. Delectable? Cunning? *Her*?

'Look,' he ground out. 'I don't know how long I can keep playing the noble gentleman with you, Audrey. I did warn you it wasn't the natural me. I want nothing more than to take you somewhere right now and make love to you all afternoon. But I know I'd feel guilty afterwards.'

He uttered a gravelly laugh. 'Hell, no one is more surprised than me that I've developed this overly active conscience where you're concerned. I know it can't last.'

I hope not, Audrey thought with a bold recklessness that should have appalled her. But didn't. She had never felt so excited in her life. All she could think about was herself and Elliot, back at his place, naked, their bodies blending over and over.

Heat seared into her cheeks. Her heart-rate tripled.

He twisted in his seat and set equally feverish eyes upon her. 'To tell you the truth, my chivalry is beginning to irritate the death out of me. Why am I holding back, I keep asking myself? She's neither a child nor a virgin. If not me, it'll be someone else soon. God knows, I've never seen a peach so ripe and ready for plucking!'

He glared at her, at her flushed cheeks, her dilated eyes, her trembling mouth.

'I'll make a bargain with you,' he growled at last. 'If we both still feel this way by the time you get your driving licence, I'll take you down to my place in the snow for a weekend. Just you and me together. No skiing. Nothing but sex. What do you say?'

Audrey couldn't say a thing.

Her eyes dropped to the car floor in a frantic confusion.

'At least by then,' he ground out, 'Russell might be well and truly out of your system and I won't feel as if I'm taking advantage of you on the rebound.'

Audrey lifted her eyes slowly to stare at him. If anyone had told her a few moments ago that Elliot would offer himself to her as a lover, and that she would knock him back, she would have said they were mad.

'Well?' he prompted, somewhat testily. 'Say something, for pity's sake. It's what you want, isn't it?'

'No,' was all she could manage.

'No?' He lanced her with a fierce frown. 'What do you mean, *no*?'

She cleared her throat. 'It means no, I'm not interested in a dirty weekend.'

'A dirty weekend?' he spluttered, a slash of angry red across his cheeks.

Her nerve started to break. What are you doing, you idiot? This is no time for a holier-than-thou attitude. So what if it's only sex he's after? So what if his rather unromantic offer sent a momentary chill running through your veins? Say you'll go! Tell him, fine, a couple of days of pure unadulterated lust is exactly what you're looking for.

'You...you said I should be looking for love, Elliot,' she blurted out instead. 'Not just sex.'

'Yes, well, that was last night,' he muttered, throwing her a cynical glance. 'I think I got carried away by my gallant knight act. Today's a different story, especially with you wearing those damned tight jeans!' His gaze dropped to her thighs—and between—where the denim fitted her like a second skin. 'Look, Audrey, you can't expect——'

Elliot broke off when cars behind them started blowing their horns. The lights, it seemed, had long turned green. He muttered something under his breath and the car leapt forward, not altogether smoothly.

'This is ridiculous,' he began grumbling under his breath. 'I knew I shouldn't get mixed up with you. I knew it was a mistake. Maybe you're not a virgin but you *are* still a child, a silly naïve little child, playing at being a woman, tying me up in knots and then——'

'Elliot!' she screamed as the Magna drifted and went breathlessly close to a truck in the next lane.

Now he didn't just mutter. He swore outright, reefing the Magna across a gap in the oncoming traffic and shooting up a quiet side-street. Wrenching the car over to the kerb, he brought it to a shuddering halt, snapping off the ignition key with an angry twist of his hand. He turned to Audrey with a face like thunder.

But he didn't say another angry word.

For Audrey was hunched there, her face like a ghost. She was trembling like a leaf, shaking so hard that her teeth were rattling.

'Oh, God,' he groaned. 'I forgot about your accident. I'm sorry. Hell, I'm a damned idiot! Here... Come over here, love...'

He undid both their seatbelts and gathered her shuddering body into his arms as best a man could in the front of a car these days.

'There, there, you're fine now,' he soothed. 'We're safe... The car's stopped... No need to worry any more... Elliot's here... I'll look after you...'

It happened again. Somewhere along the line he stopped stroking her hair, stopped uttering soft words. His fingers tipped up her chin and he took that quavering mouth into his, sighing with a type of frustrated resignation.

Audrey didn't sigh. She moaned, knowing that she was making a mockery of her earlier refusal with her instantaneous body language. If she'd meant what she'd said a minute before she wouldn't be parting her lips so eagerly now, wouldn't be letting his hand move down over her breast, wouldn't be almost sobbing with pleasure as he teased her nipple to an exquisite erection.

'Elliot,' she cried, gasping for breath as she tore her mouth away.

'Mmmm?' His hot mouth merely moved across to devour her ear instead, his hand never ceasing its erotic intent. He'd somehow undone a button or two and was inside her blouse, rubbing the already rock-like peak through the silk of her bra.

'We still can't,' she husked.

'I know...'

'Stop...please stop.'

'No,' he rasped. 'Not till I get your promise to come away with me once I've taught you to drive.'

'Yes, yes. Anything. Only stop doing that.'

'I don't want to,' he groaned.

'You're not being fair.'

'Neither are you.'

'Elliot, *please*...'

He slumped back into his seat, leaving her shaking almost as much as when he had started. Neither said a word, their mutual heavy breathing gradually settling down to relative calm.

Elliot heaved one last agitated sigh. 'You're at liberty to change your mind, Audrey,' he said tautly. 'I won't hold you to a promise made under sexual duress. I'm not that much of a bastard.'

Audrey squeezed her eyes tightly shut, her head still whirling. Elliot's earlier accusations kept going round and round in her mind, about her playing at being a woman, tying him up in knots... Wasn't that what she had just done again?

Time to really grow up, Audrey, she told herself. Time to understand that there is a difference between what you want and what you can have. Life is made up of compromises.

She drew in a deep, steadying breath. 'I won't change my mind,' she said, her voice only shaking a little. 'I do want you, Elliot. I think I have, right from that first day we met.'

He looked startled when she said this. Then concerned.

'I know you worry that I'm on the rebound from Russell,' she went on quickly. 'And that's very admirable of you. But you're not my keeper, Elliot. You yourself said that the main factor in my deciding to go to bed with a man should be if *I* wanted to. Well, I certainly want to go to bed with you, more than I ever thought it possible. But desire is not all I feel for you, Elliot.'

His head jerked her way. 'For God's sake, don't go saying you love me!'

'I have no intention of saying any such thing.' Which she didn't. Did he think she would risk the little of him she was trying to win for herself? 'I was merely explaining why I didn't like your reducing any relationship between us to a weekend of sex. I want us to have more than that together. I... I really like and admire you, Elliot. You're social-smart and sophisticated and very, very sure of yourself. All the things I've never been but would like to be. I think I can learn a lot from spending time with you.'

His grey eyes were filled with a rueful irony as they stabbed over at her. 'Are we speaking generally here, Audrey? Or are we back to sex?'

She was pleased that she didn't blush too much, her mouth pulling back into a smile that was unintentionally but very definitely provocative. 'I would say I could do with quite a few lessons in that department . . .'

Elliot laughed. 'And you think I'm equipped to give them to you?'

'Very,' she rasped.

His eyes widened, then narrowed, undeniable desire sparking in their darkened depths. 'And which lesson do you want to pursue this afternoon?' he demanded hoarsely.

A heady sense of power claimed Audrey on hearing Elliot's thickened tone, at seeing his arousal. If such a man as this wanted her so badly she *had* to be a desirable woman, a woman worth waiting for.

'I think, Elliot,' she said with her newly discovered self-confidence, 'that your original idea was best. I'll learn to drive first. And then . . . we can move on to other pursuits.'

He looked floored. 'My God, you've certainly come a long way overnight! I know I said I wanted you to take charge of your own life but don't take it too far with me, my sweet,' he warned darkly. 'You might find you have a tiger by the tail.'

He glared at her for a moment, then suddenly threw back his head and laughed. 'Hell! Who would have believed it? Checkmated by a mere novice at the game. I dare say I have no option—being a *gentleman*,' he said with a look that should have sent a warning prickle up her spine, 'but to give in graciously. Might I add, though, that you're going to learn to drive in record time? Even if we have to be at it morning, noon and night!'

# CHAPTER SIX

'AMAZING!' Elliot exclaimed. 'Simply amazing.'

'Yes, it is, isn't it?' Audrey said quite smugly.

Only six days had passed since that memorable Saturday, and already she could drive confidently in traffic. And now, this morning, she'd successfully done a reverse park without putting a single wheel wrong.

It certainly had come as a surprise that, with all her past nerves and fears, she had proven to be such an excellent driver. Though Audrey suspected Elliot had something to do with it.

After he'd made his warning edict about teaching her morning, noon and night, he'd immediately done an about-face and taken her back to his place for coffee, saying that her first driving lesson could wait till he'd found out the exact nature of the accident she'd been involved in.

Audrey had been tight with tension at finding herself alone with him so soon after his explosive reaction to her proposal, but Elliot didn't touch her in any way. On the contrary he handled her with a professional and rather impersonal kindness—as she imagined a psychiatrist might act—and soon, Audrey found herself relaxing and telling him what had led up to the accident that had killed her mother, how her father had been driving at the time—a powerful sports car—how he'd had an argument with her mother about money and had been taking his temper out on her by driving far too fast.

It had been raining and they had skidded on a corner, slewing at breakneck speed into a telegraph pole. Her mother had been killed instantly. She herself had been very badly hurt. Her father had escaped with a bruise on one elbow.

Elliot, while sympathetic about the accident and her fears relating to driving, finally commented that she might be less nervous behind the wheel than beside it. He calmed her with the thought that driving herself was another way of having control over her own life and that confidence in driving was relative to being skilled at it. Which meant being taught well in the first place.

And he proved to be a very effective teacher, taking each progressive step very slowly, using profuse praise and encouragement every time she did something right, and defusing her instant fluster with a teasing remark if she didn't. Nevertheless, when, a few days later, Audrey found her hands and feet and eyes co-ordinating with an incredible smoothness, they'd both been astonished.

Of course, her lessons had been frequent and intense. They'd spent most of Sunday on it, then Elliot had picked her up every day since for an hour before work and every afternoon for another hour afterwards. This morning—Friday—had been her hardest test yet, for it had been raining slightly, bringing back memories of her accident. She'd come through, however, with flying colours.

'You'll be ready for your test soon,' he said, and darted her a meaningful look.

Her heart missed a beat.

He hadn't touched her all week, yet every minute they spent together carried an intensifying sexual awareness. On both sides.

Sometimes, when she was on the end of one of Elliot's devouring glances, Audrey would begin hoping he was falling in love with her. But she always quickly dismissed such foolish thoughts.

Elliot had given her no reason to believe his desire was rooted in anything but a strong sex drive that hadn't been satisfied lately. Even with her hair up and wearing subdued colours, Audrey was still no stunner, certainly not the type to enslave a man against his will. Nevertheless, she could see that a man of Elliot's class and style liked his bed-partners to have an exclusivity about them. Audrey believed that her relative inexperience rather appealed to him.

But she wasn't so sure it would after the event. While the delay in consummating their desire had heightened the tension between them, it had also fuelled Audrey's doubts about her ability to please Elliot in bed. It was hard to dismiss Russell's hurtful comments, particularly since they were true. She *had* been awkward and shy and inhibited once he got her clothes off. She'd also failed to find any pleasure in the act itself. To her, it had been disappointing and embarrassing and just plain messy.

Maybe it would be the same with Elliot? Even if he managed to bring to life the woman she seemed to be in her fantasies, how would this woman compare with the other women who'd been in Elliot's life? His wife might have been plain, but Audrey felt sure she must have been a very sensual woman. Older women *were*, weren't they? One only had to look at Lavinia.

'I'll organise a test for you early next week,' Elliot informed her. 'That way, if you fail, you can take another one later in the week.'

'Perhaps we shouldn't rush into a test just yet,' she said, worried she might not be as confident with a stranger in the car as she was with Elliot. 'There's no real rush, is there?' she added without thinking.

His glance was reproachful. 'Don't turn into a tease, Audrey. You know damned well there's a rush. Another week of this and I'll be climbing the walls. There's just so much jogging and cold showers a bloke can put up with.'

'Oh...' She blushed fiercely. 'I...I didn't realise it could get that bad. I guess I'm somewhat ignorant about men and their bodies.'

'That's not such a bad thing to be,' Elliot gruffed. 'If I wanted a promiscuous little raver, I wouldn't be here with you now.'

They both fell awkwardly silent. Audrey glanced over at him just as he looked across at her. When a slow sexy smile creased his mouth, she felt her mouth go dry.

'In a way it's rather fun, this waiting,' he confessed. 'Like a child counting off the days till Christmas.' His eyes narrowed as they travelled over her body with flagrant intent. 'I'll enjoy unwrapping you, Audrey, as much as any boy with a bright new toy.'

Audrey's face flamed. As usual, Elliot was very evocative when talking about sex. But much as her arousal was instant and compelling, she couldn't discard a certain dismay at being likened to a toy, nor the insidious thought that children tended to discard their toys a few days after Christmas.

'When... when are you planning our weekend in the snow?' she asked in a husky voice.

'One week today. We'll leave on the Friday, after you finish work. Unless, of course, you can get an early mark.'

She licked very dry lips. 'What if I don't pass my driving test?'

'We'll damned well go anyway,' he said forcefully. 'If I didn't have to attend those stupid races tomorrow I'd probably have given in to temptation and taken you this weekend. Now get this chariot going again before I start getting ideas!'

'How are the driving lessons going?' Edward asked as he walked past her desk half an hour later.

'Great.'

He stopped at the door that led into his office and looked back at her, frowning. 'I hope I'm not going to lose you, Audrey. You're a very good secretary.'

Audrey swelled with pleasure. *She* believed she was a good secretary, but it was the first time her boss had ever said so. 'Why should you lose me? I'm not going anywhere.'

'Men like Elliot Knight don't let their wives work,' he stated matter-of-factly.

Audrey sucked in a startled breath before laughing, somewhat drily. 'Heavens, Edward. You're as bad as Father. He keeps asking me when I'm going to make an announcement. Elliot and I are just good friends,' she finished with that old hackneyed excuse.

Her boss gave her another thoughtful look. 'A man doesn't teach a young lady to drive because he wants to, Audrey. He usually has some ulterior motive. Has it ever occurred to you that Mr Knight might be interested in your money? After all, he's already had one rich wife.'

Audrey stiffened with outrage. Really, Edward could take his lack of tact too far sometimes. 'I don't think that——'

'I apologise for being blunt,' he interrupted, 'but I knew your father wouldn't warn you.'

Audrey was side-tracked by this statement. 'Why...why wouldn't he?'

Edward turned and walked slowly back towards her desk, briefcase in hand. 'Because he doesn't think there's anything wrong with a man marrying a woman for her money.'

Audrey felt a tightening in her throat.

'You're an attractive young lady, Audrey,' her boss went on more kindly. 'Much more attractive than you've ever given yourself credit for. Though you've really blossomed lately. You deserve better than the Russells of this world. Incidentally, you might like to hear I fired Russell yesterday.'

Audrey gasped with shock.

'Caught him pilfering car stock. Can't have that. Diane's handed in her notice as well.'

'Diane? But surely she wasn't stealing as well, was she?'

'No. But she seemed to have a disruptive influence on a certain valued member of my staff. I subtly suggested a week or so back that she might be happier elsewhere.'

Audrey didn't know what to say. She had no idea her boss had even noticed—or cared—about her happiness.

Edward's smile was full of a surprising warmth. 'As I said, Audrey, I don't want to lose you. Besides,' his smile widened with that cheeky charm he could turn on when he wanted to, 'I'm looking after my own job here. I can well see you running this company one day.'

She was startled. '*Me*?'

'Yes, you. You have a flair for administration and organisation. You also have an instinct for machines. You know more about the inner workings of the computers and printers and copiers we distribute than anyone else around here. Heck, you even fixed your own typewriter the other week with your own little hands. I was most impressed. I'll bet you're turning into a damned good driver.'

Her chin lifted. 'Yes...I am.' There was pride and confidence in her voice.

Edward nodded sagely. 'Good. Just one thing, though. Don't be too quick to give your heart to your instructor.'

When he went to walk off, Audrey jumped to her feet. 'Edward!'

'Yes?' he said, turning back with a serious face.

'Why did you say that? About Elliot? Do you know something I don't know about him?'

'Not at all. But I get the impression you don't know nearly enough either. What of his family, his background, his past? What has he told you about them?'

'Not very much,' she admitted slowly. Nothing at all, she realised with a sickening jolt.

'Then isn't it time you started asking questions, before it's too late?'

Edward's advice rolled around in Audrey's mind all day. She didn't believe for a moment that Elliot was after her money. If he had been he would have pursued her from the start. Nevertheless, she conceded she should know more about the man she was going to go to bed with in just over a week's time. Love didn't have to be *that* blind.

By the time Elliot pulled up outside the office shortly after four-thirty, she felt far too uptight for a driving lesson.

'Elliot,' she said, as soon as she climbed into the Magna, 'do you think we could give the driving lesson a miss for today?'

His glance was penetrating. 'Sure. Any particular reason?'

'Yes, I...' She broke off, swallowing. All of a sudden she couldn't do it, couldn't give Elliot the third degree she'd been intending to. Maybe she was a coward but she just didn't want to find out anything that could prevent their spending the following weekend together. She knew it was weak and stupid of her but she just couldn't help it.

'I—er—I've made an appointment at the hairdresser's,' she invented in desperation. 'Since you're picking me up for the races at eleven in the morning, that doesn't give me enough time to go tomorrow, so I thought I'd go this evening. They stay open till nine on a Friday night.'

'Ah.' He shot a worried look over at her. 'What are you going to do with your hair?'

'I'm not sure yet. I'll probably get it cut, then have some of this burgundy colour stripped out.'

'Mmmm. Yes, I guess that would look OK.'

'I wasn't asking for your approval,' she said quite sharply.

This brought another glance. This one rather puzzled. 'My, my, aren't we pernickety this afternoon? Bad day?'

'Not at all,' she lied with a tone that gave her away. 'Edward told me Russell's been fired and Diane's leaving. I couldn't be happier.'

'So I see...' Elliot's tone was very dry.

She refused to look his way, even though it sounded like he didn't see at all. And if he did, he was seeing it all wrong. Did he think she was upset that Russell was gone? God, she was thrilled! She never wanted to see that bastard again. She was angry, however, angry with herself for not having the courage to tackle Elliot with a few simple questions about himself. What was she afraid of? Elliot had never been anything but honest with her. OK, so he didn't like talking about himself. A lot of men were like that.

'Which way to your hairdressing establishment?' Elliot asked somewhat brusquely.

'Just drop me off down the main street of Newport, next to the newsagent's.'

There was a small salon tucked away in an arcade there that Audrey had walked past a few times. It was rarely full and she felt sure she could be fitted in without an appointment. Now that she had made such an excuse, she saw no reason not to go through with it. It was what she intended doing some day anyway. Why not tonight? 'I'll catch a taxi home afterwards,' she told him.

'Are you sure you don't want me to come and pick you up?'

'No, I have no idea when I'll be finished. You go home and study your form guide. I don't know one end of a horse from the other so I'll be looking for you to give me some tips tomorrow.'

His chuckle was wry. 'You might be broke by the end of the day, though I guess that won't worry the heiress of Modern Office Supplies. I read in the *Financial Times* only this morning that it's an up-and-coming company, profits growing each year.'

The hairs on the back of Audrey's neck prickled. 'Oh? You make a habit of reading the *Financial Times*, do you?'

He shrugged. 'I haven't for a while, but I thought it was time I got back to work. Friday's paper is full of good jobs.'

Audrey fell silent. Was Elliot going back to work because he needed the money? Had he perhaps already run through his wife's?

More questions abounded on the tip of her tongue. Where do you come from? Who were your parents? How did you meet your wife? Did you *really* love her?

Damn it all! Why couldn't she just come out with a few of them? It was quite normal and natural for her to want to know more about him.

'This do?' he asked, pulling over to the kerb.

She blinked. 'Oh, yes . . . fine.' She opened the door and went to get out when Elliot's hand on her shoulder stilled her.

She turned slowly to look at him. God, but he was devastatingly handsome. Handsome and sexy, but too darned enigmatic for her peace of mind. 'Yes?' she asked, her big brown eyes projecting a pained dismay at her thoughts.

'Nothing,' he said softly. 'Just this . . .' And he leant over and kissed her.

It was their first kiss since last Saturday and she couldn't help wondering if it was a kiss with a purpose, designed to cloud not clarify, to seduce not soothe.

But oh, the feel of his lips on hers was heaven. She sighed into his mouth, meeting his tongue halfway, welcoming its rather leisurely but exquisitely arousing exploration. Her hands clutched at his shirt and before she knew it, she was pulling him closer... closer...

It was Elliot who ended the kiss, Elliot who sent her off aching for him, Elliot who waved a cool goodbye, grey eyes glittering in a face carved like granite.

She watched him drive off, suddenly consumed with real alarm. Had his kiss been a deliberate ploy to keep her under his spell, because he had seen her slipping away from him? Did he have an ulterior motive in continuing to see her? Other than sex, that was. Marriage, maybe?

But that was far-fetched and ridiculous! She was imagining things. Edward had put ideas into her mind, ideas that had no basis in fact. Elliot might not be a saint but he had his own brand of honour and she loved him. Loved him and wanted him. What was more, she was going to have him. And nothing, absolutely nothing, was going to stand in her way!

# CHAPTER SEVEN

WHEN Audrey arrived home shortly after nine that night she was caught going upstairs to her room by a scowling Lavinia striding across the foyer. Her stepmother looked even more livid when she glanced up and saw Audrey's hair.

Audrey knew why. Her hair looked terrific. Gone was the hideous frizz, replaced by a sleek, chic bob that swept across her forehead from a side-parting to curve softly around her ears and jawline. Gone was the burgundy colour, replaced by a warm golden blonde, lustrous and flattering to her fair complexion.

'Good God!' Lavina exclaimed derisively, black eyes flashing. 'What *have* you done to your hair?'

Audrey was ready for her in every way. 'Nothing,' she retorted blithely. 'It was all my new hairdresser's doing, actually.'

'Very smart, Audrey,' the other woman sneered. 'I must say your turning twenty-one hasn't improved your manners. Or maybe it's the company you're keeping. But I do think you might inform us when you're not coming home for dinner. Poor Elsie cooked for you for nothing!'

'I tried to telephone from the hairdresser's,' Audrey defended. 'But the number was always engaged. Besides, you told me you and Father were going out to dinner tonight and Elsie always goes to a movie when you do that. I didn't realise I was putting anyone out.'

'Yes, well, your father had to stay home to take some business calls from overseas.'

'I could hardly have been expected to know that, surely, Lavinia.'

'Know what?' asked a male voice.

Lavinia totally changed her demeanour at her husband's sudden appearance. All aggression dissipated, a feminine coyness in its place. 'About our staying in tonight, darling,' she continued. 'It seems Audrey didn't go out with Elliot after all. She went to the hairdresser.'

Warwick Farnsworth gave his daughter a smiling scrutiny. 'She certainly did. Audrey, my dear, you're transformed! I would have walked past you in the street and not recognised you. You look so different as a blonde. Older... more sophisticated.'

'Why, thank you, Father. I like my new look too. I'm not so sure Lavinia does, though.'

He gave his wife a frowning look. 'I don't know how she couldn't. And I see you've been clothes shopping.' He nodded towards the various plastic bags she was carrying.

'Yes. I'm off to the races tomorrow with Elliot. I thought a new outfit was in order.'

Warwick looked surprised. 'The races? Horse-racing or car-racing?'

'Horse-racing. Didn't Lavinia tell you? Elliot owns a part share of a horse, a filly named Little Girl Pink.'

'No, she didn't.' There was a tightening of his mouth as a sharp glance passed between him and Lavinia. It was the first inkling Audrey had ever had that their relationship might not always be sweet sailing. But she found it hard to feel sympathy for her father in this. He'd married one woman for money and another for sex, neither very admirable reasons. He'd made his bed with Lavinia. Now he had to lie in it.

'I must go,' Audrey said, and hurried up the rest of the stairs. 'I have a lot to do before tomorrow.'

Which she did.

Her hours at the hairdresser's had proved a real boon. Not only had she been delighted with the way they'd done her hair, but the owner of the shop— a warm, friendly woman—was a good friend of the lady who managed the boutique next door. They'd got talking, and soon Audrey was being shown outfit after outfit as she sat under the drier. By the end of her stay she had chosen several new dresses and suits, along with matching accessories. She'd also been persuaded to have her face made up by the salon's beautician, and had subsequently purchased the whole range of products the girl had used on her.

But she really needed to practise what she'd been shown before she forgot how to do it for herself.

Audrey dashed into her room and dumped all the bags on her bed. Finding the one with the make-up in it, she carefully arranged all the jars and bottles and tubes and brushes on her dressing-table, then sat down to stare in the mirror and admire her new look.

Of course the main change *was* her hair, with its softening effect. But she did so like the way the beautician had pencilled more definition into her eyebrows. As for her eyes... They looked large and appealing with the multi shadings of brown around them, not to mention the lashings of mascara.

Her hands lifted to trace over cheekbones she hadn't known she had. But there they were, highlighted with a sweep of blusher from her cheek to her temple. Her mouth looked less girlish too, the dark lip-liner and shimmering gloss inside producing a lushly full effect. All in all, Audrey thought she looked... Dared she think it? *Sexy*? Or was that going too far? Maybe she should settle for sophisticated. Yes... That would do. Sophisticated.

She wondered what Elliot would think of her.

Butterflies churned in her stomach.

She dived on to her bed, rolling over on to her back and laughing happily.

Elliot...

She bounced off the bed, feeling another burst of wild elation as she caught sight of her reflection once more.

'You won't get away from me now, Elliot Knight,' she cried, and hugged her new self in delight.

'Good God!' Elliot exclaimed, startled eyes sweeping over Audrey as she stepped out on to the landing, shutting the front door firmly behind her.

'Don't you like it?' she asked coyly, well aware of the admiring flashes in his astonished gaze.

'What's *it*?' he laughed. 'Your hair, your face, or that smashing dress?'

She flushed with sheer pleasure. 'The lot, I guess.'

His gaze zoomed down the row of black buttons that went from the deep V neckline down to the hem of the sleek cream woollen dress, then back up to her swinging blonde hairstyle and perfectly made-up face. Before he could say another word, she lifted the black straw picture hat she was holding and placed it saucily on her head. 'And what about this?' she smiled, even more confident now.

'Fantastic!' he said, shaking his head in awe.

He looked pretty fantastic himself, in a light grey three-piece suit and white silk shirt. There was none of the stubble he'd been sporting all week, his very male jaw-line satin smooth. Every lock of his thick dark hair was in place as well, slicked back away from his incredibly handsome face and fine grey eyes.

This time next week, came the unexpected thought, and Audrey's stomach did a somersault.

'Would you have recognised me if you passed me on the street?' Audrey asked swiftly, needing a distraction from X-rated thoughts.

'Of course!'

'Oh, yes?' she scoffed lightly. 'My father said he wouldn't have.'

Elliot's smile was far too sexy for words. 'Honey, I'd recognise those eyes of yours no matter what you did to them. And that mouth...' One hand reached out to touch the shining bronze gloss with a soft fingertip. 'Keep close today, darling,' he whispered. 'I don't want to smash some daring gambler's teeth in when he tries to chat you up. Now put that hat of yours under your arm and come along. Your future awaits.'

'My future?' She froze for a second and blinked up at him.

He laughed. 'The races, then.'

But Audrey had thought he meant something else for a moment. Edward's warnings popped back into her mind again and she darted Elliot a worried glance. She didn't think he'd planned it all along, but was it possible that, having encountered her re-vamped appearance, he *was* thinking about marrying her for her money?

She felt shaken with the realisation that she didn't automatically reject that idea.

'I still can't get over how great you look as a blonde,' he said as he handed her into the passenger side of the black Saab.

Audrey's smile felt stiff to her but Elliot didn't appear to notice. He seemed in a very good mood all of a sudden, which worried her all the more. Though perhaps she was misreading the whole situation. Perhaps he just felt better about presenting a better-turned-out Audrey Farnsworth to his friends today.

She didn't know, would never know anything much about Elliot if she just kept on sitting there with her stupid mouth shut. Say something! Ask him a few questions! Get some answers!

But she couldn't seem to find the right words. Or the courage to say them.

Elliot chatted to her on and off all the way to Rosehill.

And revealed absolutely nothing.

Audrey had no idea how he did it. Or why.

She comforted herself with the thought that he couldn't *force* her to marry him if that was his plan. She might love him like crazy, *and* be prepared to go to bed with him. But till she knew a lot more about him, that was as far as their relationship would go.

The race-course came into sight, the expanse of green grass looking odd against a background of factory chimneys and roofs. Audrey had never been to Rosehill before. She had gone along to Randwick once on Derby Day, when her father had been a guest of one of his many millionaire acquaintances. The races seemed to be full of people like that. Extremely wealthy owners, or rich businessmen out to impress clients with a day's lavish entertainment at the sport of kings.

She wondered if Elliot's friends would be like that.

Such thoughts began to make her even more agitated about the coming afternoon. Looking physically better had not turned her overnight into a social animal, and one successful dinner party with people she knew was not the same as having to converse with perfect strangers. She had the awful feeling she could easily revert to her former shy, tongue-tied adolescent-like self when confronted by strangers.

'Elliot,' she blurted out at last.

'Mmmm?'

He seemed distracted, his attention on getting his car safely through the busy car park. An attendant was directing the line of vehicles into various places, though they weren't all being obedient. The car in front of them actually started reversing. Audrey sucked in a panicky breath. Elliot gave an impatient growl, wrenching the wheel sideways and shooting into a neat spot between a dark blue Mercedes and a silver Rolls. Though she was relieved to be safely stopped, the sight of the stylishly dressed people spilling from these cars only increased Audrey's nerves.

'Elliot,' she repeated.

'Yes?' He turned off the engine and retrieved the keys before he turned towards her.

'You haven't told me anything about these people whose private box we'll be in. Who are they?'

'Co-owners of the horse. Nice people. You've no need to worry.'

'But I *am* worried,' she said tautly. 'I'd at least like to know their names and a little bit about them. I mean . . .' She shrugged helplessly.

He twisted round to pick up his form guide and binoculars from the back seat. 'Mr and Mrs Nigel Evans will be our hosts. They're the only ones I know really well. Nigel was Moira's publisher. His wife's name is Yvonne. The others are a Mr and Mrs Bill Dayton. Wife, Joyce. He owns a printing firm. And another couple named Gregson. Mike's the husband but I forget his wife's name. Helen, I think. Actually, they're more Moira's friends than mine,' he said. 'Little Pink Girl was hers. Horses, you see, were one of her many passions.'

Audrey tried to ignore Elliot's wife having 'passions', and taking a deep breath, found herself giving him a firm look. 'No, I don't see. How could I? I know nothing about Moira. Or your marriage. I've been wondering when you intend enlightening me. Before or *after* we've been to bed?'

Audrey was astonished how proud of herself she felt now that she had spoken up, even though her hands were shaking underneath her hat.

'Neither,' Elliot said curtly.

'Why not?'

He spun round to lance her with irritated eyes. 'For God's sake, Audrey, I don't see what my marriage to Moira has to do with us. It's dead and gone. Just leave it that way, will you? Hell, it's taken me a year to get over my guilt where Moira's concerned as it is!'

'G...guilt?' she stammered. 'Guilt over what?' The possibilities were endless...

'Over her death,' he explained tersely, and Audrey felt sick with relief. 'I always blamed myself for being away for so long. I knew she hadn't been well and I shouldn't have gone.'

'Gone where? Where did you go?'

'Overseas. To Europe. I'd been asked to help plan the courses for the following year's world skiing championships. The downhill and slalom runs.'

Audrey gaped at him. He noted her expression with a rueful reaction. 'I did say I ski'd. Fact is, I used to do it professionally. I'm quite well known in international skiing circles.'

'Oh...I...I didn't know.'

'Why should you? Skiing doesn't get much publicity in Australia and my competitive days were a few years back now.'

'But I should have asked you about yourself before now,' she said, frowning.

'Yes...perhaps you should have.' He darted her a close look. 'Are you asking now?'

Her heart quavered but she held his eyes reasonably steadily. 'Yes...'

'*Right* now?'

'Yes.'

His sigh was drily amused. 'You do pick your moments, Audrey, my love.' He glanced at his watch. 'I suppose I could spare you enough time for a brief résumé. Let's see... I'm an only child. My father deserted my mother when I was only a baby. My mother died just after I graduated high school. I won a scholarship to university, and ski'd during the holidays. Became a lawyer, worked and saved, took two years off when I was twenty-seven to ski full-time. At twenty-nine I smashed my right knee and had to give up racing. I came back to Australia, returned to work, met Moira at a party. We started living together pretty quickly, eventually married. You know the rest.'

'You... left out all the other women,' Audrey said, holding her breath. 'The ones you said you had till you were twenty-nine.'

He gave a dry laugh. 'My dear sweet Audrey, if I enumerated all my past conquests, we could be here forever.'

When she looked shocked he gave her a sardonic glance. 'I did warn you. And I make no apologies. None of the women I bedded were sorry afterwards. Why should *I* be? Have I shocked you?' He laughed again. 'It seems I have. Good. You do have a bad habit, sweet thing, of looking at me with rose-coloured spectacles. Believe me when I say my one claim to virtue where women are concerned is my behaviour so far with you.'

She stared at him. Did that mean he *had* married Moira for her money? Or that he'd been unfaithful to her?

'If it's in danger of slipping,' he growled, eyes raking over her, 'then you can blame yourself. You shouldn't be looking so gorgeous and sexy today...'

Audrey thought she was ready for his kiss this time, thought she would be able to hold down her responses. But her pulse had already quickened before his lips actually made contact, her insides tightening in readiness for the sweep of sensation that would inexorably claim them.

She moaned beneath the harsh pressure of his lips, the invasion of his tongue. Her heart pounded. Her mind whirled. This was love at its worst.

Compulsive, obsessive, crazy. It didn't want to listen to reason. Or warnings. Even when those warnings were being uttered by the very object of that love.

Elliot was the one to pull away. 'I think we'd better be heading inside the track,' he said with a dry laugh, 'or we might not get there at all!'

# CHAPTER EIGHT

AUDREY got through the next half-hour far better than she'd thought she would, given the circumstances. Not only did she have to contend with social nerves, but a hefty dose of sexual agitation. Elliot helped with the first, she supposed, plying her with a couple of glasses of white wine as soon as they made it into the private box with its well-stocked bar across the back. But he kept the latter at fever pitch by remaining glued to her side, one of his hands always either on her waist or curved over her hip as introductions were made.

Still, he was right about one thing. Moira's friends *were* nice. They weren't at all snobbish or affected as some wealthy people were, and accepted her quite naturally as Elliot's new girlfriend, something that surprised her. She would have expected them to resent her seemingly taking Moira's place so soon after her death. The publisher, Nigel Evans, and his wife, Yvonne, both in their late forties, were particularly pleasant to her, the other two couples keeping mainly to their own company.

When Elliot departed with Nigel shortly before the first race to place a few bets, leaving the two women together, Yvonne turned to Audrey with a ready smile.

'It's wonderful to see Elliot getting out and about again after Moira's death,' she said. 'And with someone so nice and *young*. Nigel and I have been terribly worried about him. I suppose you know he took his wife's death very hard.'

Audrey said she did, but her mind was still puzzling over the woman's emphasis on the word *young*.

Yvonne distracted her with a friendly hand on her wrist. 'Would you think me rude if I asked if you and Elliot were serious about each other?'

'Good heavens, no!' Audrey exclaimed automatically. 'We ... we've only known each other a couple of weeks.'

The other woman nodded. 'I see. Well, that *is* early days yet. Still, I know Moira would have been pleased if you were.' She gave a small laugh. 'Don't look so surprised, my dear. Moira was not a possessive woman. She would have wanted Elliot to marry again, not go back to his earlier lifestyle. He certainly was one for the ladies before he married Moira.'

'Yes, so I've heard,' Audrey agreed.

'*Have* you? Who told you?'

'Elliot did.'

'That's not like him. He's usually so closed-mouthed about himself. Truly, if Moira hadn't been a close friend my curiosity about him would never have been satisfied. He must think a lot of you to tell you about himself.'

Audrey's heart sank. She didn't know so very much.

'Have I said something wrong?' Yvonne asked, frowning.

'No, no,' Audrey hastened to soothe. 'It's just that I would like to know a little more about Elliot. But one doesn't like to pry.'

'Nonsense! We women should stick together. I'll tell you anything you want to know. Just fire away!'

How could she resist? 'Was . . . was Elliot's and Moira's marriage a love-match?'

Yvonne frowned. 'Now that's a hard one. It certainly was on Moira's part. She was mad about him. As for Elliot? Mmmm . . . Naturally there was a lot of speculation about his having married Moira for her fame and money. But I never did go along with that. Elliot had a top job as a lawyer with a big company. And he'd had plenty of fame himself with his skiing successes. Besides, he did seem to care for her. Though I would hesitate to call his affection real love.' She sighed. 'Moira always said he was loath to trust a woman with his complete heart after what his mother did to him.'

Audrey blinked. 'Pardon?'

'You don't know about that? Tell me, my dear, what *has* Elliot told you about his growing up years?'

Audrey's whole insides contracted. 'Not much. I know his father deserted the family when he was just a baby and that his mother died soon after he graduated.'

'That's a rather skeletal version. His father did desert him. But so did his mother, when he was eight.'

Audrey must have looked shocked.

'She was an alcoholic,' Yvonne explained. 'Elliot was made a ward of the state and put into various foster homes, but he grew into an antisocial teenager and ended up in a boy's home. One of those charities which specialise in providing holidays to underprivileged children took him down to the snow when he was fifteen and he was discovered to have a rare talent for skiing. You do know about his skiing, don't you?'

'A little . . .'

'He was a freak at it, apparently. Not to mention quite a budding genius at his schoolwork. The patrons of this particular charity provided a scholarship for him to go to university to study law, *and* be taught skiing in his spare time. Their investments were rewarded by Elliot's topping his university at law and becoming a world-class skier at the same time.'

'Goodness!' Audrey exclaimed, truly astonished.

'It's said he could have been the world champion downhill racer if he'd lived in Europe and not here in Australia with its limited facilities and competition. As it was, he was doing quite well, always finishing in the top ten. That and his looks won him a lucrative royalty contract with a European ski clothes company.

'Not that Elliot told Moira all this personally,' Yvonne went on with a sigh. 'She'd gleaned most of it over the years from other sources long before they met. Because Moira, you see, was one of his patrons.'

Audrey was speechless.

Yvonne was unlikely to ever be similarly indisposed. 'She told me that the night she first met him down at an end-of-season skiing party at Perisher Valley he was heartlessly turning the head of every woman he was introduced to in the room. He had quite a reputation as a stud, especially with the type of older woman who only wanted sex from a relationship. Divorcees . . . Widows . . . Career women . . . Unhappy wives . . .'

Audrey felt a chill ripple through her.

'But then, life on the international skiing circuit *is* scandalously fast,' Yvonne tossed off blithely. 'Moira found his Don Juan behaviour drily amusing from a distance but when he started trying to cynically charm her, with her sitting there in a wheelchair, she saw red.'

Yvonne gave a light, remembering laugh while Audrey was trying to come to terms not only with the image of Elliot as a hardened rake, but the even more startling image of Elliot's wife in a wheelchair.

'Believe me when I say Moira looked a serene lady,' Yvonne continued. 'But she wasn't. She told me she tore strips off him, dressed him down in no uncertain terms in public, then froze him out for the rest of the night. Apparently, he was intrigued. And possibly challenged. Moira was no lightweight in the brain department. He rang her the next night and their relationship began...'

'Was...was Moira always in a wheelchair?'

'No. She had her good times and bad times. MS is like that, it seems. She used to spend a lot of time down the snow because cold apparently lessens the symptoms. Whatever the reason, shortly after meeting Elliot she went into remission for a couple of years. But a few weeks before she died it flared up again. Still, she was always very brave, very strong. She didn't let anything beat her. But you know... I often think it's as well she passed away when she did...'

'Why do you say that? Was...was Elliot being unfaithful to her?'

Yvonne shrugged. 'I have no evidence of it, but it's hard to see him resisting all the women who kept throwing themselves at him. Oh-oh, here he comes with Nigel,' she warned. 'Don't say I told you any of this, for pity's sake. Elliot would be furious, and so would Nigel. He says I talk too much.'

'I won't breathe a word,' Audrey said tautly, her mind reeling.

'You two look as thick as thieves,' Elliot smiled, curving a possessive arm around Audrey's waist. She stiffened. But when he smiled back down at her, eyes warm and full of desire, any worries about Elliot's character seemed to vanish. All she could think of was right here and now. And, right here and now, she wanted him like crazy. Nothing else mattered. Besides, it wasn't as though he'd ever tried to deceive her with his intentions. Or lack of them!

'We were discussing the chances for the coming race,' Yvonne said smoothly.

'And what do you fancy, Audrey?' Elliot asked.

Her eyes flashed *you* at him, before she could stop them.

He raised an eyebrow and leant close to her ear. 'Minx,' he whispered. 'We're here to watch Little Girl Pink race. Nothing more!'

'What . . . what race is she in?' she asked, heart thudding away.

'Race three. It goes off at one thirty-five.'

'And do you think she'll win?'

He shrugged. 'The trainer doesn't think so, but Nigel tells me he's a cautious man. Here's my form guide. Read it and make up your own mind. Far be it from me to influence you,' he added, a teasing gleam in his eyes.

With cheeks colouring, Audrey fell to studying the various information, happy to get her mind off what Elliot could do to her body without even trying.

'From what I can gather,' she said after a minute or two, 'Little Girl Pink's being ridden by an underrated though competent jockey. They say here that with her light weight and excellent barrier position she has a better chance than a lot of the others.'

'Spoken like a true gambler!' Nigel joked.

'Not only that,' she grinned, 'the jockey's wearing cream and black. *My* colours.'

'Oh, well, in that case,' Elliot mocked in dry amusement, 'I shall follow your expert advice and to hell with the trainer!'

Audrey thought he was only jesting so she was startled when later he lashed out with a thousand dollars each way at twenty-five to one on the filly. It made her ten-dollar fun bet look paltry by comparison. The one soothing aspect was that it squashed any theory about Elliot needing money.

Audrey was surprised by the excited tension that seized her when the horses started coming out on to the track. She spied the number eleven on the saddle cloth of a pretty chestnut with a white blaze down her face. 'I see her!' she squealed, and almost choked Elliot when she grabbed his binoculars to watch the filly going round to the barrier stalls.

'Oh, she's beautiful,' she bubbled. 'And very toey.'

Elliot took the glasses from her, rubbing his neck ruefully where the strap had been. '*Toey*? That's a very horsy phrase for a girl who claims not to know one end of them from the other.'

Audrey looked sheepish. 'I heard Nigel say that about his selection in the first race.'

Everyone laughed.

'Let's hope our filly does better than that particular nag,' Nigel said drily. 'I think it's still running.'

'I hope so too,' Audrey agreed, eyeing the betting tickets in Elliot's breast pocket with growing agitation.

Little Girl Pink didn't win. But she did run third, to everyone's delight. There was a lot of hugging all round. Elliot's place ticket returned him over five thousand dollars on the Tote, whereupon he gave Audrey a thousand dollars. 'To replace your loss,' he said.

'Oh, but I can't accept!' she exclaimed, face still flushed with excitement. 'I only lost ten dollars.'

'Go on,' he insisted. 'Take it. Be corrupted. I might make you earn it later,' he added in a hoarse whisper.

Audrey's cheeks scorched. She felt both aroused and shocked at the same time. Perhaps he was only joking but she wasn't used to this type of sophisticated banter. When he saw her embarrassment, he gave her a quick hug. 'You're delightful, do you know that? So delightful,' he said, nuzzling her ear, 'that I find I cannot wait after all.'

'I'm sorry, folks,' he directed aloud to the rest of the group, 'but Audrey and I have to leave. I'm taking her down to the snow for the rest of the weekend.'

Audrey just caught her startled gasp in time. For a second all she felt was excitement, but then a not so pleasant realisation took hold of her, a realisation of what Elliot had just done. She bit her bottom lip, her newly emerging self-esteem telling her that this wasn't right, that Elliot shouldn't be allowed to make up his mind for both of them off the cuff like this, without consulting her, without so much as a by-your-leave. Much as she wanted him, she really couldn't meekly accept such behaviour. She had to make a stand over this, or all the personal gains she had made over the last week would be wasted.

But she didn't like to make a fuss in front of these nice people. She would wait till they were back at the car.

'Do you have to go so soon?' Yvonne complained. 'I was so enjoying your company.'

Everyone concurred with that.

Elliot remained adamant, however, and soon, he was urging an increasingly resentful Audrey through the crowd and out into the car park. She had to clamp her hat tightly on to her head with her free hand or it would have flown away, so fast were they going. Truly, what did he think he was going to do, have her in the car park? Heavens, but he must think she had no mind of her own! Or did he imagine he was so devastatingly attractive that she would go along with whatever he wanted, whenever he wanted it? In love with him she might be, but a wishy-washy ninny she was no longer. Russell had cured her of that!

They reached the Saab and as Elliot bent to open the passenger door with his key she spoke up. 'You shouldn't have done that, Elliot,' she started shakily, but with inner conviction. 'You...you should have asked me first.'

He straightened, his expression both taken aback and irritated. It was the expression of a man who liked his own way and who didn't expect a girl like

Audrey to thwart him. Her whole chest contracted as she waited for him to answer.

You should have kept your big mouth shut, you fool! she told herself. He'll probably take you straight home now, drop you off and sail off into the sunset, never to be seen again!

When he nodded slowly, a wry smile coming to his face, her relief was cataclysmic.

'You're right,' he agreed. 'I should have. It was presumptuous and arrogant of me. I'm sorry.'

'That's all right,' she said, and felt a satisfaction she had never known before. She had stood up for her principles and won a concession.

He looked deep into her eyes, taking her hat off and placing it on the hood of the car before gathering her into his arms. 'Will you come with me, Audrey?' he murmured, and bent to brush her lips with his. 'Right now...' His lips parted slightly with the next brief kiss. 'And stay with me all weekend?'

His lips descended once more and Audrey thought of nothing for the next minute or two. In truth, even when his mouth lifted from hers she was still incapable of putting two sensible thoughts together.

'You haven't answered me yet,' he said softly.

'I'm...I'm not on the Pill, you know,' she blurted out.

'Meaning?'

'You...you'll have to...to...'

He smiled gently and hugged her. 'Of course.'

She expelled a trembling sigh against his chest. 'I'm going to be horribly nervous, Elliot.'

He started stroking her hair. 'That's nothing to be ashamed of, darling.'

She quivered under the endearment and the soothing touch of his fingers gliding over her hair.

'People are looking at us,' she rasped.

'Let them.'

'Oh, I do so want you, Elliot.'

She actually felt him tremble and it was the most marvellous moment for Audrey, to think she could make him respond so.

'Shall I find a motel for us nearby?' he asked in a thickened tone.

She was tempted. But only for a moment. A motel conjured up images of grotty one-night stands and adulterous rendezvous. She wanted her first time with Elliot to be somewhere extra private and very, very special. It was worth waiting a few hours to have the right setting.

But she understood that men didn't always want to wait. Elliot's own words came floating back, when he'd said that when it came to sex frustrated men could be like animals, wanting what they wanted when they wanted it. Her mind cringed away from his added words that they didn't always care whom they had it with.

She hated the thought that she might only be a female body to him, only a means of satisfying his physical needs. Suddenly, it was important to her that he wait those few hours. Maybe it wouldn't prove a thing, but she refused to relinquish the idea once it had taken hold.

Slowly she eased herself out of his arms and looked up. 'I . . . I'd rather go down to the snow,' she said nervously. 'Do you mind?'

His laugh was rueful. 'Of course I mind. But if it's what you prefer . . .'

She nodded.

'Then so be it. But I must warn you——'

'Y... yes?'

'We're going to break the record from here to the Snowy Mountains.'

She stiffened, frightened by the thought of them hurtling off some ice-slick road at a madcap speed.

'Damn, I forgot,' he groaned, seeing her instant alarm. 'OK, we'll break the record for getting from here to Jindabyne while *not* exceeding the speed-limit. Fair enough?'

'Fair enough,' she smiled, sighing.

He was as good as his word. But he kept the needle hovering on the limit right from the start, and soon they had passed the city limits and were on the expressway, heading south.

'Can I put some music on?' she asked after half an hour. Elliot didn't seem in the mood to talk and the scenery had a sameness about it that was hypnotically boring. Audrey had never been on this particular highway before, and it seemed to bypass the towns.

'Sure. Pick what you like. There's a wide selection in the dash.'

She selected the score to the Tom Cruise movie, *Top Gun*, and slipped it into the player, leaning back and closing her eyes as the pulsing beat of the music throbbed into the car.

'Try to have a sleep,' Elliot suggested.

She couldn't, of course. Who could? She did, however, pretend to, turning her face away from him and staring blindly through the passenger window. Eventually they did move on to a more interesting piece of road that skirted a lot of low-lying ponds or dams. A sign said it was called Lake George.

Funny sort of lake, she thought. They flashed past the turn-off to Canberra and were soon high-tailing it to Cooma. There was no stopping, no slowing down, no chit-chat.

Eventually, the sun sank low in the sky, casting a yellow-gold glow over the far hills before dropping suddenly behind, plunging the countryside into a cool grey dusk. A full moon appeared in the charcoal sky. The darkening scenery began to blur, and, finally, Audrey did fall asleep.

A hand gently shook her shoulder. 'Audrey... We're here.'

She sat bolt upright, and glanced around. They were in a cavern-like garage that had obviously been carved out of a hillside, solid rock forming all the walls bar the one they'd driven through, even though the roller-door was already shutting behind them.

A shiver ran through her.

'Come on,' Elliot said, rolling stiff shoulders and reaching for the door-handle. 'We need to get up-stairs and turn the heating on.'

Audrey climbed out of the car in a type of numbed state. Here... They were here... Oh, God...

'Up this way,' Elliot called and walked across the cement floor to where an internal staircase ended in a trapdoor in the ceiling of the garage. Elliot went up first to attend the deadlock. 'Can't be too security-conscious around here,' he explained as he inserted a key. 'Empty holiday homes are a real target for break-ins.'

The trapdoor led into the most enormous living area Audrey had ever seen. It too must have been partly underground, though only the back wall was hewn rock this time. The side-walls of the room were windowless and white, but the wall she found herself facing was completely glass. Clouds must have formed to cover the moon, for it was too dark to see any real view, just the hint of tree-tops and a few spots of lights shimmering down in the distance. Obviously they were high up, possibly on the side of a mountain or a hill. Audrey could also tell from the silence that they weren't on a main road or near other houses.

She glanced around, taking in the luxurious furnishings from the thick grey carpet to the black television and video unit to the dark red leather sofas and chairs. A huge black circular combustion heater rested majestically in the centre of the room, its black funnel disappearing into the white ceiling.

Audrey swung her gaze to the well-appointed kitchen which was starkly white and sectioned off from the rest of the room by a breakfast bar attended by three black leather stools. To its left, partially in front of the plate-glass window, sat a glass dining table with six red leather chairs marking out the circumference of its circular shape.

Everything in the room was either grey, white, black or red. The effect was very dramatic and very male, leading Audrey to believe that this had always been Elliot's place, never Moira's. It made her feel better, somehow.

'Make yourself at home,' Elliot suggested. 'I'll just turn on the heating and then I'll get us something hot to eat and drink.' He walked over and turned on some switches on the far wall. 'Damn, but it's freezing in here! I think I'll light the fire as well.'

Audrey watched him attend efficiently to the fire, all the while aware that she was becoming more tense with each passing second. Any confidence she had acquired recently also went down the drain. She felt awkward and plain again. She just knew she was going to be a failure at lovemaking, that Elliot would end up thinking her as big a bore as Russell had.

She bit her lip and walked over to pretend to look at the view, and could just make out what she thought was a large body of water. Jindabyne Lake, she supposed.

'Pull the curtains, will you?' he asked. 'It'll help keep the warmth in.'

The curtains were heavy black silk. Audrey yanked the cord and they shot across, shutting out the world. Without knowing why, she glanced up at the ceiling.

'Yes, there's another floor above,' Elliot confirmed. 'Two bedrooms with en suites. Hopefully getting warmer by the minute. One of those far doors leads to the stairs. The other's a powder-room. I imagine you want to use it. I know I do. You first, though. When you come back sit down over here near the fire,' he suggested, nodding towards one of the large red sofas that flanked the heater. 'I'll leave the glass door open so that you can get some heat straight away. I'll get us some food as soon as this is going. Will lasagne and coffee do? I'll microwave it.'

'Sounds great,' she said, and moved hurriedly towards the powder-room. All of a sudden she wanted to use it very, very badly.

It wasn't long, however, before they were both sitting in front of a crackling fire, eating and drinking and looking like they didn't have a care in the world.

How appearances could be deceiving, she was thinking as she forked the last of the lasagne into her mouth. She was literally scared to death. She hadn't tasted a single mouthful of her food, neither could she remember a word she'd said in answer to Elliot's innocuous remarks. She placed the plate down on the side-table next to her and picked up her coffee. It too seemed tasteless, but she drank it down in deep gulps, sighing deeply when it was all gone.

Perhaps Elliot sensed her apprehension, for suddenly he put his own food aside and slid along the sofa. He took the empty coffee-mug out of her hands, leaning across her to put it down as well.

'Enough of this procrastinating,' he rasped, and pulled her down on to the sofa with him.

# CHAPTER NINE

ELLIOT was kissing Audrey before she could say a word, rolling her under him, pressing her down into the soft red leather with the weight of his body. His hands lifted to hold her face, keeping her mouth a firm prisoner for his increasingly passionate kisses. He groaned, parting his legs to fall on either side of her own, bringing his lower body in forceful contact with hers.

Audrey felt a momentary panic at the stark evidence of his desire, pressing so urgently between her thighs. He felt so much bigger than Russell. Nerves fluttered once again in her stomach. Would she disappoint him? Yet at the same time her body leapt in automatic response to his awe-inspiring need, and she arched up against him.

He gasped away from her mouth, rolling to one side and almost falling off the sofa. 'God, Audrey!'

She cringed at the reproach in his voice. Feelings of utter inadequacy and failure crowded in. She was hopeless, useless, stupid!

'No, no,' he said gently, and cupped her fallen face to kiss it softly all over. 'I'm not annoyed with you. It's just... I'm very, very excited, love.' His hand stroked her forehead, her cheeks, her mouth. 'You're so lovely and I've been wanting you so much. Do you understand what I'm saying?'

She blinked up at him, her heart pounding, her mind dazzled. Yes, she thought in a whirl of wonder. 'I've been wanting you too,' she murmured, and gave a little shiver.

'You can't possibly be cold,' he teased.

She shook her head.

He drew in then expelled a ragged sigh.

'I want to take your clothes off, Audrey. I want to see you, touch you . . . Right here. But if you'd rather, we could go up to the bedroom . . .'

Her mouth went dry, her heart-rate going up a notch. 'Here would be fine,' she rasped.

He bent to kiss her again, distracting her quite successfully with his mouth while his fingers smoothly tackled the buttons on her dress. Soon a number of them were undone, as was the front clasp of her bra, and his hands began doing marvellous things to her breasts.

Too marvellous. The blood roared around in her head, her heart going so fast she thought it must disintegrate. But when he slid her skirt up around her hips and starting divesting her of all her clothes from the waist down, she gasped away from his mouth.

'It's all right,' he soothed, and sat up to complete what he had started till she was naked underneath from the waist down. And while Audrey was not ashamed of her body—it was adequate enough—she still felt shy under Elliot's direct gaze. She would never have let Russell look at her so boldly. Never!

But then, she loved Elliot. Really loved him. And he was looking at her so admiringly, and with such genuine desire.

'You have a beautiful body, Audrey,' he said, and bent to kiss one taut pink tip, then the other.

Audrey thought she would die from pleasure.
'Oh, Elliot,' she quivered.

He lifted his head to stare down at her, a slightly
bemused look on his face. 'The man must have been
mad,' he muttered. 'Didn't he know what he had
in you? Couldn't he *see*?' He took her mouth again
quite fiercely, lying her back, his hands moving
underneath the gaping dress to her naked body,
searching for and finding her most intimate places
and showing her that Russell had known as much
about a woman's body as the Dark Ages had about
classical music.

When she started moaning Elliot sat up abruptly, pulling her with him into a sitting position
where he took off her dress and threw it aside before
returning to similarly dispose of her already dys-
functioning bra. For a long moment he just stared
down at her totally nude body, grey eyes like molten
steel, then he was reefing his tie from his throat and
yanking it over his head. 'Help me, Audrey,' he
commanded huskily, eyes darkening.

She did so, all their hands trembling as they
stripped him with little finesse and no regard for
what his clothes might have cost. Jacket, shirt, belt,
socks, shoes. When it came to his trousers they had
to stand up, Audrey's heart racing as he finally
stood before her in all his naked male glory. She
stared up at him, revelling in the lean, well-honed
muscles that had carried his superbly proportioned
frame at break-neck speed down snow-covered
mountainsides.

Her eyes dropped nervously to his manhood,
which was proudly erect, and as formidable as she
had suspected. She swallowed convulsively.

'I must attend to certain matters, Audrey,' he rasped, 'before I forget.'

A moment later he turned round, and she stepped forward and pressed her naked, aroused body against him. He groaned in reply, and, scooping her arms up around his neck, captured her mouth in a fevered kiss. His hands roved over her bare back, then dropped to the soft womanly flesh of her buttocks. He began pressing her closer and closer, moving his aroused flesh against her. She could feel the building frustration in his hands and his mouth, though it was no greater than her own. She wanted him and she wanted him now!

When one hand slid down to grasp her left leg, lifting it high and giving his hardness access to the soft moist flesh between her thighs, she moaned with relief. The feel of it rubbing against her was incredibly exciting. But soon it wasn't enough. Not nearly enough. At the point when she was about to beg him to take her, he lifted her whole body slightly off the carpet and entered her with a single forceful thrust.

Audrey gasped away from his mouth, eyes wide with astonishment and pleasure. He groaned then smiled at her through heavy-lidded eyes. 'I hope that feels as good for you as it does for me.'

'Yes,' she shuddered. 'Oh, yes...'

Hands curved securely around her buttocks, both her feet now off the floor, he turned and lowered himself into a sitting position in the middle of the sofa, settling her firmly astride him. As her bent knees sank further into the soft leather, so did his flesh sink further into her. She closed her eyes and shuddered again with emotional and physical ecstasy...

Elliot ... her love ... her lover.

'Make love to me, Audrey,' he exhorted thickly.

Her eyes flew open, her heart fluttering wildly. *Her*, make love to *him*? But ... but *how* exactly? This was a new experience for her, a new position, a new ...

'Like this?' he urged, and, grasping her hips, moved them in a voluptuous circle, then slowly up and down.

'Oh, God,' he exhaled raggedly.

'Oh, God' was *right*, she thought, amazed by the sensations that had rocketed through her.

Yet she felt unable to do it on her own. It seemed too ... wanton. Elliot repeated his urgings, not once, but many times, and soon Audrey was caught up in a wild world of escalating pleasure and tension that knew no such thing as inhibition. She gradually forgot her shyness, or fear of being thought wanton. Everything became frantic inside her. She had to move faster, and faster, her head tipping back, her lips parting in panting readiness for the end of this crazily erotic journey. For it wasn't far off, she knew. It *couldn't* be!

And then there it was, an experience that was almost frightening in its intensity, gripping at her flesh excruciatingly as every nerve-ending seemed to balance on a knife-edge before abruptly shattering, seemingly splitting her asunder. Gasp upon shuddering gasp broke from her throat as the sharply electric sensations reverberated around Elliot.

He cried out too, and she felt his release, felt the warm pulsating flood as his body blended even more totally with hers.

She slumped forward, her cheek against his shoulder, her chest still heaving. It took ages for her heartbeat to slow down and by the time it did a heavy blanket of contentment was already beginning to envelop her. Elliot's arms moved to slide around her back, holding her close.

'You're fantastic,' he said softly. 'Do you know that?'

'I never realised,' she murmured against his shoulder.

'Realised that you were fantastic?'

'No. That sex could be like that.' She let out a long, shuddering sigh, pressing soft lips to his skin.

'Not sex, Audrey. Making love. We made love...'

A lump of emotion claimed her chest and tears pricked at her eyes. He was still her gallant knight... always saying and doing the right thing. What more could a woman ask for?

His *heart*? a relentless little voice whispered.

Oh, shut up, came her mental retort, fierce and angry. This is reality here, not some romantic fantasy!

Her head jerked up; she was determined not to let schoolgirl dreams spoil this time she had with Elliot. For who knew how soon it would end? He was always telling her to make her own decisions, forge her own future. Well, her future had to start with the present and the present was Elliot.

'What is it?' he asked, startled perhaps by the look of determination on her face.

'Elliot...'

'Yes?'

'How...how...' Her voice dried up, her courage failing her. Self-disgust made her look down. So much for forging her own future! She couldn't even put a voice to a simple statement of desire.

'How what?' he said teasingly. 'Come on, Audrey. Just say it. I can assure you I'm not shockable.'

A burst of spirit seized her and her head snapped up. But on meeting his dancing eyes she flushed. 'I...I was going to ask...' She gulped before going on, her voice still sounding croaky. 'How soon before we could do it again?'

His laughter was soft, his eyes sparkling as he leant forward to place a light kiss on her mouth. 'Well, you have had rather a draining effect on me, you little minx. Shall we say I'll probably be recovered by the time we've had our bath?'

Her eyes flew wide. '*Our* bath?'

'Yes, *ours*,' he said firmly, and rose, carrying her with him.

'I should ring home,' she said tautly, closing her eyes against the feelings his hands were evoking in her as he gently soaped her breasts. 'Let them know where I am.'

'Later,' he murmured. 'Now we're relaxing. Lie back.'

*Relaxing*? her aroused brain taunted. The man was mad! How could she possibly be relaxed lying naked in a bath with him, spoon fashion, his long muscular legs on either side of her? She felt like a cat on a hot tin roof!

'I...I don't feel very relaxed at this moment,' she choked out.

He chuckled drily and kissed her wet shoulders. 'You should be. Contrary to popular opinion, water is supposed to be a poor aphrodisiac for women.'

Says who? Audrey thought mutinously.

She stifled a gasp as his soapy fingers brushed once again over her nipples, which were pointing out of the bubbly water straight at the ceiling like twin mountain peaks. 'Certain parts of me are not in the water,' she reminded him in a tight little voice.

He laughed but he thankfully moved down on to her ribs and stomach, much less arousing areas of her body. Gradually, under his gentle massaging, she felt the tension unravel out of her muscles, the heat of the water and his hands performing a small miracle in her opinion. A quavering sigh floated from her lips, a sigh of relief and yes, relaxation.

'Elliot,' she murmured at last.

'What?'

'This is very nice.'

'So glad you like it,' he muttered.

'Don't you?' she asked, vaguely aware of the edge in his voice.

'I think perhaps it's time we got out.'

'All right,' she said dreamily.

He lifted her wet body from the bath, her legs and arms floppy. She actually yawned and heard Elliot laugh as though from a distance.

'I think you've carried my advice a bit too far,' he drawled, and took her back to the now well warmed bedroom, spreading her damp body out on to the deep red velvet quilt that covered the large bed. Its velvet material felt deliciously sensual beneath her naked flesh. *She* felt deliciously sensual. She stretched like a cat, her arms flopping back above her head, revelling in the feel of the warm plush pile against her water-slicked skin.

'Don't go away,' he mocked as she stretched again, and disappeared back into the bathroom for a second before returning with a large fluffy red towel in his hands.

'Where shall I dry you first, I wonder?' he murmured. 'Here?' He took one arm and rubbed it gently. Then the other. She sighed appreciatively.

'Here perhaps?' Now her legs got the same attention.

Audrey was enjoying that too, her eyelids growing heavy, till she realised the towel was going higher and higher up between her thighs. When it reached its goal her eyes shot open.

'Ah,' Elliot said with satisfaction. 'I see you've decided to rejoin the living.'

When he started rubbing the towel lightly across her stomach, then up over her breasts, a low groan rumbled in her throat. He didn't stop, however; he kept rubbing and rubbing, less gently now.

'I think you might be dry enough,' he ground out at last and threw the towel away. Audrey looked up at him with eyes dark with desire, but he just stood there, staring down at her body, spread out seductively on the red quilt.

When he reached out to run the back of his fingers over her breasts and stomach, her whole skin broke out in goose-bumps.

'You've got beautiful skin, Audrey. So soft and creamy. I could look at it forever. And touch it . . .' He stretched out beside her. 'And kiss it . . .'

His mouth bent to kiss the underside of one breast, then travelled slowly upwards to close over a nipple, drawing it in sharply, rolling his tongue over and over the tenderised peak till she made a whimpering protest.

He stopped immediately, then startled her by sliding down her body and putting his mouth where no man had ever put his mouth before. She would have died of shock and embarrassment if Russell had made such a move, but with Elliot any momentary qualms were quickly put aside, replaced by the most enthralling experience of sheer sensual pleasure.

Though this kind of pleasure had its dark side, Audrey was to find, and soon every nerve-ending in her body was electrified by what Elliot was doing, the sensations almost too sharp to be enjoyable. Her head thrashed from side to side and she began to wonder if she really wanted this exquisite agony to go on.

Yet when Elliot stopped abruptly, her only feelings were an intense dismay and disappointment. When he rolled her body away from him over on to her stomach, she groaned in protest. Till he started kissing her shoulders, moving her hair aside and running his tongue up and down the soft skin of her neck, nibbling on her earlobe, breathing warm erotic air into her ear.

She shivered convulsively.

His chuckle was low and sexy. 'I love your reactions,' he murmured. 'I love everything about you.'

She groaned in desolation when his mouth lifted from her ear, but then a lone feathering fingertip started tracing down her spine from her neck to her buttocks, and every muscle inside her sprang to attention, contracting into the most heart-stoppingly exciting knot. Her heartbeat suspended, then went mad again.

'You have a beautiful back too,' he rasped, his fingertip wandering off to trace circles over her buttocks. 'Beautiful...'

Audrey froze with anticipation when the finger returned to its initial travels, starting once again at the base of her spine and moving downwards. By the time Elliot finally reached the moistened depths of her desire, she was trembling. By the time he stroked her thighs apart, all she knew was that she had to have him inside her, no matter what.

She was utterly beyond caring when he grasped her hips and scooped her up on hands and knees, sliding into her from behind.

Her only reaction was a shuddering sigh of relief.

'Yes ... oh, yes,' she moaned when he started to move, her desire flaring madly, twisting at her insides, her fingers clutching and unclutching the quilt beneath her hands with convulsive movements. Elliot's hands were making similar kneading actions on her breasts, his breath hot in her ear as he told her how beautiful she was and how much he wanted her, how often he would take her. His impassioned words sent her wild, and before she knew it she was tumbling over into a shatteringly electric release that had her almost sobbing in bitter-sweet ecstasy.

Elliot responded with a fierce climax of his own, holding her tightly as he shuddered into her for several seconds, then drawing her down with him as he collapsed, gasping, on to the bed.

Audrey lay there in his still quivering arms, stunned by what they had just shared. The passion ... the intensity ... And the marvellous contentment afterwards, the inner peace ... It was so much more than she had ever dreamt, or hoped for. How was she ever going to survive when it was all over, when she would never be held in Elliot's arms again, never feel this peace, this joy? *How*?

Her sigh was both sensuous and sad.

'What are you thinking about?' he murmured, pulling her back into him, spoon fashion.

'That it must be wonderful to be able to do this every night,' she answered quite truthfully.

He gave a soft chuckle. 'I think that could be arranged, don't you?'

Audrey stopped breathing. Surely he wasn't going to ask her to marry him, was he?

The perverseness of her finding such an idea alarming did not elude her. Heavens, how often would a girl who was desperately in love *not* want her lover to ask her that question? Nevertheless, she didn't want Elliot to ask her. Not at all. He didn't love her and such a proposal could only mean one thing. Just *thinking* about his reason for asking sent a chill deep into her soul.

'I've been thinking,' he said, and pressed softly teasing lips over her ear, 'how would you like to move in with me, live with me?'

Audrey's heart leapt with both relief and instant excitement. She twisted in his arms, looking up into his waiting face with bright happy eyes. 'Are you sure, Elliot? I mean . . . *really* sure? I . . . I'm not the tidiest person in the world.'

His smile was sardonic. 'I don't think I'm thinking of your tidiness at the moment, sweet thing.' And, capturing her chin with his hand, took her mouth in an explosively hungry kiss.

'God, I've never wanted a woman as much as I keep wanting you,' he muttered against her swollen lips at long last. 'Every night wouldn't nearly be enough for me.'

His fevered words fired Audrey to run a bold hand down his body. 'Nor for me,' she husked, a wave of desire swamping her as her intimate touch quickly stirred him to full arousal again. 'Oh, Elliot... I do so adore the way it feels with your body inside mine. Do it again... Please...'

He groaned and pulled her under him quite roughly, wrapping her legs high around his waist and plunging forward into her hot eager flesh. Her swollen muscles enclosed around him tightly, bringing a moan from deep within his throat. 'Something tells me,' he rasped, 'that this is going to be a long... long... night.'

# CHAPTER TEN

'ELLIOT,' Audrey whispered shortly after midnight, 'I . . . I haven't rung home to say where I am. They'll be worried.' She levered her head up from where it was resting on his stomach.

'No, they won't,' he returned with cool logic, and stroked her head back down again. 'They won't start to worry till they check your bedroom tomorrow. And if I know Lavinia that won't be too early on a Sunday. You can ring them in the morning with some plausible excuse as to why you're not home. Say you stayed the night at Nigel's place, that we partied on there after the races and I had too much to drink to drive you home.'

'Yes . . . I suppose I could do that. It's just that I'm not a very good liar. They're sure to guess the truth.'

'And if they do? You're an adult, Audrey, not a child. There's nothing wrong with your having a sex life, provided it's discreet and not indiscriminate.'

Audrey flinched at Elliot's categorising what they'd been doing as her 'sex life'. Hadn't he himself said they'd been making love, not 'having sex'?

'Besides,' he added, 'they'll know soon enough when you move out of home and in with me.'

The ramifications of what she had done, agreeing to live with Elliot, hit her. What was her father going to say? And Lavinia . . .

'You're very silent and still all of a sudden,' Elliot probed softly. 'Are you having second thoughts about moving in with me?'

She sat up and pushed the hair back from her face, then lay down next to Elliot, her head on the pillow. 'No,' she said at last. 'But I don't think I'll get the family seal of approval.'

'Why? Because they know I won't marry you in the end?'

Her eyes darted sideways to him, her heart squeezing tight. For Audrey wasn't so sure any more that she didn't want Elliot to ask her to marry him. Or that he didn't love her. How could a man make love so beautifully and so often if he wasn't in love? Where did the tenderness and caring come from that made *her* pleasure his first concern, never his own? Was that the action of a man who wanted only sex? She didn't think so.

'You knew that, Audrey,' he said tautly. 'I'll be your lover for as long as you want me. But I won't marry you. I'm not the marrying kind.'

'You married Moira.'

'That was different.'

'How was it different?' she demanded to know. '*How*?'

He sat up abruptly, swinging his legs over the side of the bed. 'I won't be cross-questioned,' he threw at her over his shoulder, his voice chilling in its reproach. 'Not by you. Not by anyone. You take me as I am, Audrey, or don't take me at all. That's the bottom line.'

She sat bolt upright and simply stared at him, her heart thudding. This was an Elliot she'd never seen before, a coldly ruthless Elliot, a darkly forbidding creature. A *black* knight, not a gallant one.

For a split second she was shocked. And hurt. But then she saw the unspoken pain in every rigid muscle in his stiffly held back and knew there had to be many complex reasons why he was acting this way. It was not at all like the man she'd come to know and love. Perhaps if she probed gently...

Kneeling up behind him, she slipped her arms around his chest and hugged him.

'Elliot... I understand. Truly.'

He tensed even more.

'You're still suffering from your wife's death. I can see you must have loved her very much. But can't you also see that what we feel for each other is more than just desire?'

'No!' he denied, and slammed one fist into the other. 'You're wrong and I *won't* be responsible for fooling you!'

He twisted round and took her by the shoulders, his face hard. 'Firstly, let's get one thing straight. My marriage to Moira was an act of friendship, not romance. Moira was worried over some greedy relatives getting their hands on her estate after she died. She reasoned that they wouldn't contest a will against a legitimate husband. So to give her peace of mind—the doctors had said she couldn't live longer than five years—I married her and promised to always direct a large percentage of her royalties to her favourite charities. Which I have. I liked and admired Moira greatly, but I did not love her. I have *never* fallen in love with a woman, Audrey, simply because I'm not capable of it!'

Audrey just stared at him, eyes wide with shock and confusion and outright disbelief. A steely glitter came into his eyes when he saw her reaction, and quite deliberately he let one hand drift down to curve deliciously over her breast. 'You think this means you love me?' he rasped, his thumb arousing the nipple quite ruthlessly. 'Not necessarily, Audrey. Any more than this means *I* love *you*.' And he picked up her hand and held it to him. 'This is desire, not love. Surely you've learnt the difference by now!'

He put her hand aside, every muscle in his jaw clenching down hard. 'If you still think you love me then it's better we terminate our relationship right now. You'll get over me soon enough once I disappear from the scene. And you certainly won't have any trouble finding someone else, looking as you look nowadays.'

Audrey stared at him, trying desperately to see beneath the tough surface to the human being beneath. She could understand that anyone with his unfortunate background would have difficulty with trust and love. This unwillingness to fall in love was shown by his earlier womanising tendencies, the love-'em and leave-'em attitude Yvonne had told her about. Moira must have been one special lady to capture as much of his affection as she had.

But couldn't he see that he had changed, that the man who'd been so kind and sweet to her *was* capable of a deeply caring love?

His stubborn blindness in this matter frustrated the life of her. *I've* been hurt too, she wanted to scream at him. The answer *isn't* to cut oneself off from feeling too deeply for risk of being hurt again. The answer is to open one's heart, to keep searching for love. Russell was a disaster. But I didn't give up. I kept looking and I found *you*, my darling. And I have no intention of letting you get away. I'm going to make you see all this if it kills me!

Meanwhile . . .

Audrey gulped down the lump of emotion that had gathered in her throat, recognising that she had to lighten the situation at this point in time or risk losing Elliot altogether.

The smile she painted on her face was mischievous and carefree. 'My, who would have thought you'd be such a worry-wart? So what if I've fallen for you? It's not as though I want to *marry* you. I'm too young. *You* told me that. I want to have fun for a few years. And I want to have it with *you*. So you can stop this bad-tempered act. You won't get rid of me that easily!'

He stared down at her, uncertainty in his face.

'Had enough rest yet?' she teased, cocking her head on side. 'You do realise we haven't reached that quota you whispered to me earlier in the night.'

He shook his head, then laughed. 'Whatever am I going to do with you?'

'You mean you don't know?' She gave a mock sigh. 'And there I was thinking you knew everything there was to know about this. It just goes to show. You can fool some of the people all of the time, and all of the people some of the time. But not——'

She yelped when he pulled her roughly into his arms and down on to the bed. 'I think I should warn you,' he growled, a wicked smile coming to his mouth as it descended, 'that I find challenges almost as irresistible as I find a certain naked blonde!'

'Lavinia? Is that you?'
'No, lovie, Elsie here.'

Audrey breathed a sigh of relief into the telephone. 'Are Father or Lavinia up yet?'

'Haven't seen hide nor hair of them. Still, it's only half-past ten. Where are you, lovie? I had no idea you were even up yourself. Have an early driving lesson, did you?'

Audrey was consumed with even more relief at this ready-made alibi. 'Yes, that's right,' she lied more happily. 'Elliot wanted to get an early start before the Sunday traffic built up. I'm over at his place now having some brunch. I thought I'd better ring and let you know where I'd got to and that I won't be in for any meals today. Elliot's taking me out for the day.'

'You're really getting along with that young man, aren't you?'

'Er—yes.' Her stomach fluttered as she glanced at Elliot, moving around the kitchen, making breakfast. He looked wonderfully rakish in a black bathrobe and nothing else. She wasn't wearing much more herself. A large red towel, sarong-style, covered her nakedness from breast to thigh. Another was wrapped around her freshly shampooed hair.

'He's a terrific person,' she complimented, catching Elliot's eye. He took a mock bow.

'It certainly is nice of him to teach you to drive. That takes a lot of patience.'

'Oh, yes, Elliot's *very* patient.'

His head snapped round, one eyebrow lifting. He mouthed, 'No, I'm not. Get over here and help me, you lazy little devil.'

'I suppose you want me to pass on the message about your being out today to your father and Mrs Farnsworth?' Elsie offered.

'Yes, please.'

'Will do. See you later, lovie.'

'Bye, Elsie.'

'See?' Elliot grinned as she hung up. 'No trouble.'

'You're corrupting me,' Audrey laughed.

Elliot turned back to the bacon and eggs, his expression sardonic. 'I'm not sure who's corrupting whom any longer.'

She levered herself off the stool and came round the breakfast bar to stand behind Elliot, running her hands across his broad shoulders. He was so beautiful, she thought. So very very beautiful ...

And he was hers. For now.

'Is that your idea of helping?' he tossed over his shoulder at her.

She slid her arms around his waist, laying her cheek against his back. 'Yes,' she sighed.

'You're an affectionate little thing, aren't you?'

'I don't know. I've never had anyone to be really affectionate with before.'

'Not even Russell?'

She slowly straightened, pulling away from him. 'Why bring him up?' she asked tautly. 'You know I can't stand that man any more.'

'Just checking.' He glanced round at her. 'Hey, don't look so serious. What happened to that girl who just wanted to have fun?'

'She does have a serious side occasionally.'

'Good. Then put some bread in the toaster. We have some serious bacon and eggs ready here very shortly.'

She laughed.

'Who's going to do the cooking when I move in?' she asked once they were seated on opposite sides of the breakfast bar, tucking into the food.

'You'll be sorry if you say me,' she teased. 'I've never cooked a proper meal in my life.'

'Then *I* will attend to such matters.' He gave a pompous bow of his head over his bacon and eggs. 'Your trusty house-boy at your service, madam.'

'And what other...services...do you provide, o, trusty house-boy?' she asked, getting into the spirit of the game.

'Madam!' His affronted tone was a splendid imitation of the stuffiest English butler. 'I don't know what you mean.'

'You could have fooled me. You gave me a complete itinerary of your abilities last night. And very proficient you were too.'

'Madam seemed to master the various techniques quite quickly herself. But then, of course, she's a very quick learner.'

'True...but I'll need a refresher course at least every other day.'

'Oh, no, I don't think that would do at all.'

'You don't?'

'Definitely not. Let one day go and things are likely to slip.'

'Really? I thought it was a bit like riding a bike. Once you got the hang of it, you——'

'Madam! The things you say. I'm blushing.'

'And I'm the Queen of England.'

He looked over at her and they both burst out laughing.

It was a glorious day. Both mad and marvellous. Once, they started making crazy love out on the balcony, but when the icy winter air endangered certain areas with frostbite they quickly moved inside on to the carpet, where a warming pool of sun filtered through the plate-glass window. Elliot kept her in stitches as he continued the farce of a pretend mistress-servant relationship, though she decided she could certainly get used to the way he waited on her hand and foot. Not that his cooking was *cordon bleu*. Mostly, they ate microwaved snacks.

Four o'clock saw them making a reluctant return to the car for the trip back to Sydney, though it was a far cry from their trip out. They played childish games most of the way, making words out of number plates as well as trying an old favourite in 'I spy'.

They rolled into McDonald's at Goulburn on the way and made utter pigs of themselves with burgers and fries and thick shakes.

'I seem to have worked up an appetite somehow,' Elliot said with droll humour as he devoured a second Big Mac.

'I wonder why?' Audrey countered with feigned innocence.

'Don't ask me. I've been flat on my back most of the day.' He raised an eyebrow at her and she coloured.

'Is it my fault you don't like the missionary position?'

'That's because I'm not a missionary.'

She spluttered back into laughter and Elliot joined her. They were still laughing as they climbed back into the waiting Saab.

'Don't come in with me,' she requested when they pulled up outside the infamous Farnsworth steps shortly after ten. 'I want to break the news on my own.'

'You'll pack tonight, though?'

She smiled and kissed him. 'Even if I have to stay up half the night.'

'I'll be here at seven-thirty in the morning for your driving lesson. Put your luggage in the Magna. I'll come in a taxi.'

'I'll be ready.'

'Don't let Lavinia upset you!' he called after her as she climbed out.

'Not in a million years,' she returned confidently.

But she was far from confident once Elliot had driven off and she was alone. All her new-found courage seemed to have gone with him.

Her father and Lavinia were still up, watching television in his study. Audrey walked in with a nervous 'hello'.

'I thought I heard someone at the door,' Lavinia said, her black gaze widening as it flicked over Audrey's cream woollen dress. 'Heavens, you're still wearing the same clothes you wore yesterday. Don't tell me you didn't come home last night at all, Audrey? I thought you told Elsie that——'

'I spent the night with Elliot,' she interrupted in a rush of resolve. 'You might as well know.' She directed her words more at her father than Lavinia. 'I love him, Father, and he . . . he cares for me. He's asked me to live with him and I'm going to. *Please* don't make a fuss. I'm twenty-one and you can't really stop me.'

Warwick Farnsworth said nothing for a long moment. Then he nodded slowly. 'If that's what you want, my dear . . .'

Audrey trembled with relief and happiness.

'Warwick!' Lavinia burst out. 'How can you take this so calmly? Why, the man's years older than

Audrey. For all we know he might be a con-man, a gold-digger, a——'

'He's a perfectly respectable lawyer. Not to mention a world-famous athlete,' Warwick returned calmly. 'He's also a lot richer than my daughter. Do you think I didn't check him out?' He stood up and walked over to take his daughter's hands in his. 'You do what you think is right, Audrey. You deserve some personal happiness after Russell. Edward told me about him. I just wish I'd known earlier what a snake-in-the-grass he was. But he always presented himself very well, you must admit. Though not a patch on your Elliot, of course...'

'I don't believe this,' Lavinia muttered from behind him. 'He won't *marry* her, you know! Not if he's already rich.'

Audrey saw the flash of irritation in her father's eyes as he swung on his wife. 'Some people do marry for reasons other than money, Lavinia,' he said sharply.

'*Do* they?' she taunted acidly.

A slash of red burnt across her father's cheeks. Audrey wanted to hit Lavinia for being such a bitch.

Her father said nothing, however. But his eyes were hurt. He drew himself up proudly, thereby gaining more respect from Audrey than he had in his entire lifetime. 'Yes,' he said staunchly. 'The trouble is, it isn't always realised till it's too late.'

There was a second's electric silence.

'Anyway, we're getting off the point here,' he went on. 'As an adult, Audrey's entitled to find love wherever and however she sees fit. From what I have seen, Elliot Knight seems a decent man. I don't think he'd deliberately hurt her.'

'Is that so?' Lavinia snapped. 'Well, it just goes to show what a pair of naïve fools you both are! The man's nothing but a philanderer, a...a roué! Audrey's just a novelty to him. He's been enjoying himself playing at Pygmalion with her, though now he's probably moved on to *The Story of O*! No doubt he's got her——'

'That's enough!' Warwick roared. 'I'll be pleased if you'd keep your disgusting opinions to yourself in future, thank you, Lavinia. I would also like to talk to my daughter. *Alone*!'

Lavinia's face went bright red. 'Very well,' she ground out. 'But don't say I didn't warn you, Audrey. As soon as you begin to bore Elliot in bed, he'll replace you with someone a little more...experienced. Mark my words!' And, giving them both a contemptuous look, she swept angrily from the room, banging the door behind her.

Audrey felt dreadful. 'I'm so sorry, Father,' she began shakily. 'I...I didn't mean to cause trouble.'

He shook his head wearily. 'It's not your fault, my dear. Lavinia is... Well, she isn't a very happy person lately. She and I haven't been getting along. But that's not your worry. However...' He hesitated and Audrey's insides tightened.

'You *are* quite sure about going to live with this man, are you? Lavinia does have a point about his being a lot older than you. And a lot more experienced...'

'I'm sure,' she lied.

'So be it, then,' her father sighed. 'Now off you go to bed, my girl. You look a little...worn-out,' he finished with the flicker of a wry smile.

She felt the heat zoom into her cheeks. 'Yes, I am a bit. I have to pack too.'

Her father looked startled. 'So soon?'

'I'm moving out in the morning.'

He sighed. 'I'll miss you...'

His sincerity touched her and she gave him a fierce hug. 'I'll visit,' she promised.

'I hope so...'

Audrey went up to bed with mixed emotions, not at all sure now she was doing the right thing. Why was it, she agonised, that other people could put such doubts into her heart? She knew Lavinia was jealous, but still her words had cut deep into her optimism, her hope for the future.

Was sex all there would ever be to her relationship with Elliot?

She hoped not. Surely once they were living under the same roof, day after day, week after week, there would be much more time for them just to talk, to get to know each other on many levels. Their relationship would grow and when it did Elliot would realise the depth of their attachment for each other.

Audrey began to pack, her steadying thoughts having brought a return of excited anticipation. Tomorrow, Elliot was coming for her. Tomorrow, she would become a part of his life. Tomorrow...

But when she finally lay down to sleep Lavinia's warnings kept coming back to haunt her. Then when she drifted off Audrey's dreams were nightmares of horror and insecurity. In one, Elliot was standing over her with a whip, and in the background, Lavinia was laughing and mocking her as she cringed away from Elliot like a frightened animal, fear a real and tangible thing crawling over her skin. Elliot was taunting her, telling her she was a naïve little fool, that young women bored the hell out of him, that his only pleasure with her was to laugh at her inadequacies. Then he told her he wanted a 'real' woman, turning to begin making love to Lavinia in front of her.

Audrey woke, trembling and wretched. But when Elliot arrived on time, smiling as he gently kissed her mouth, all her doubts disappeared, replaced by a feeling of the utmost love and trust. He was her Elliot, her knight in shining armour. He would never betray her.

Perhaps it was as well that the future lay hidden from her eyes.

# CHAPTER ELEVEN

'I THOUGHT you said you and Elliot weren't serious,' Yvonne remarked as she drew Audrey into the kitchen. 'Isn't living together serious these days?'

Nigel had rung Elliot over business during the week and invited him to dinner for the Sunday night, extending the invitation to Audrey when he'd been enlightened over Elliot's new living arrangements.

'It's only been a week,' Audrey hedged. 'And we've no intention of getting married.'

Yvonne began pouring more potato chips into the empty bowl she'd carried in. They were still on pre-dinner drinks and munchies. 'I must say I'm still a little surprised,' she said, 'though it was obvious from seeing you together at the races that Elliot was very taken with you. Who knows?' she laughed. 'Maye he's finally got over his penchant for older women!'

Audrey gave a forced laugh. 'I certainly hope so.'

The other woman gave her a sharp look, then sighed. 'You're terribly in love with him, my dear, aren't you?'

Audrey flushed, glancing nervously over her shoulder to see where Elliot was. But he was busily chatting away to Nigel in the living-room.

Yvonne patted her hand. 'No need to be embarrassed. Elliot is one gorgeous man. I only hope . . .

Oh, nothing. You're only young once. Just enjoy yourself with him while it lasts.'

Resentment burnt inside Audrey. Why did everybody think her relationship with Elliot would never go anywhere?

Her resentment quickly changed to an honest pessimism. Why not? Elliot himself didn't think so either. And, even though they'd only been together for a week, there was no sign of that deepening of their relationship that Audrey had secretly hoped for, no deep and meaningful talks, no simple companionship.

Elliot's interest in her remained strictly physical. He couldn't seem to get enough of her, driving her to work every morning at the last second, picking her up at lunchtime to bring her back home where they'd inevitably end up making love for the whole hour. Even her driving lessons had suffered, with frequent clinches distracting them. How she'd passed her driving test she didn't know. But she'd sailed through without making a mistake.

Their nights were just as hectic as the days, though at least Elliot tried to create the illusion of a real romance. He spent every afternoon preparing a candle-lit dinner which he served up to her with great panache, insisting they dress up for the occasion.

Then afterwards...

Audrey sighed. She was just as bad as he was in a way. For she was always more than willing, always terribly aroused by the time dinner was over and Elliot began slowly to undress her.

But she hated every free hour of their lives being seemingly controlled by their insatiable desire for each other. She wanted more. The trouble was, Elliot didn't. She knew it, and so did everyone else.

'Does that sigh mean that everything's not perfect in the Garden of Eden?' her hostess probed carefully.

Audrey's smile was bleak. 'I just wish Elliot would let me inside his mind occasionally. I never really know what he's thinking.'

'God, if only I had a dollar for every time Moira said something like that!' She gave Audrey a sharp look. 'Do you mind me talking about Moira? Please say so if you do.'

'No, not really,' came the surprisingly truthful admission. 'She sounds as though she was a terrific person.'

'She had her bad side. Like everyone. She could be very stubborn. And quite brutal with her opinions. But she had high expectations of people, regardless of their excuses for acting badly. All her friends tried to live up to those expectations because somehow you felt you were letting her down if you didn't.' Yvonne laughed. 'She accused me of being an inveterate gossip. And I am! But I wasn't around her, believe me!'

'And what did she think of Elliot?'

Yvonne laughed. 'That he liked his own way far too much, and that he needed a woman to stand up to him!'

It was just a tossed-off remark, but it set Audrey thinking. She was still thinking when she and Elliot arrived home.

As soon as he shut the door he drew her into his arms. She stiffened. 'Something wrong, sweet thing?' he frowned down at her. 'Come to think of it, you've been rather quiet tonight. I thought you'd got over your social nerves.'

She pulled away from the temptation of his embrace and began walking towards the bedroom. 'I have, by and large. But I...I have a splitting headache.'

She *felt* rather than *saw* his silent stare.

'This isn't one of those headache jokes, is it?' he said at last, following her into the bedroom.

She pulled a nightie out of the drawer that held her lingerie, then turned to face him. 'No. It's for real. I'm sorry, Elliot, but I don't feel up to making love tonight.' Audrey tried not to look guilty, for she didn't have a headache, even though her mind did feel stressed. She did, however, feel compelled to see how Elliot would handle their relationship without sex for a day or so, to force him to just *talk* to her.

He glared down at the nightie clutched to her chest. 'Obviously,' was his dry remark. She hadn't worn a thing to bed all last week.

'If you like I could sleep in the spare room,' she suggested, then waited in trepidation for his answer.

Please don't let me do that, Elliot, she willed. Please tell me you want me beside you, anyway.

She held his eyes and actually saw them harden. 'You're lying to me, Audrey. *Why*?'

'I...I'm not.' Despite all her efforts at control, a guilty heat claimed her cheeks. 'I do have a headache,' she insisted, all the while knowing she was making a mess of this. 'If you don't believe me then I can't help that!'

'I don't believe you,' he said coldly. 'Enjoy your night in the guest room.' Without another word he strode into the main en-suite bathroom, slamming the door behind him.

'You're looking peaky,' Edward said to her the next morning at work. 'Not like last Monday. My God, when you walked in here, looking like a young gorgeous Grace Kelly, I almost fell off my chair. Today, however...' He pursed his lips in disapproval. 'Perhaps it's just as well you're having your insurance check-up later this morning. Maybe the doc will be able to find out what's wrong with you.'

'Oh, goodness, I forgot about that,' Audrey groaned, thinking of all her good intentions to make up with Elliot at lunchtime. Her night in the guest room had been horrific, and breakfast even worse. Elliot had tried to break the ice and she, like a childish idiot, had accused him of not caring about her at all, of only wanting her for sex.

He'd given her one of those long, unreadable looks he was good at, then told her that wasn't true. He did care about her. If he'd wanted a woman 'just for sex', he'd have chosen someone better suited, someone a little more mature, not a pouting sulky irrational child who deserved her bottom spanked.

She'd retorted that he was nothing but a self-centred, selfish, stupid sex maniac who ought to take a good look at himself before he ended up a lonely old man. Whereupon she had stomped out of the house and driven herself to work very shakily, peak-hour traffic and her nerves almost making her run up the back of a bus on one occasion.

'What time's my appointment?' she asked Edward.

'Eleven-thirty.'

An appointment at that time in the city meant she wouldn't be able to see Elliot at lunchtime. She groaned. He would probably think she was making up an excuse not to see him at all. Her hand shook as she reached for the phone to call him. Dear heaven, what a muddle she was in!

But Elliot didn't make any accusations when she told him, his indifferent tone upsetting her more than if he'd ranted and raved.

'I'm really sorry about this, Elliot,' she babbled on regardless. 'It's unavoidable. The whole staff here has a medical check-up every couple of years and the appointment's been made for ages and I can't really——'

'For pity's sake, Audrey,' he cut in impatiently. 'You don't have to answer to me.'

'But...but of course I do!'

'Why?'

'Because I...I feel rotten about what happened and I wanted to talk to you about it, explain how I felt. I...I don't want you to think I don't want you any more.'

'I don't think that,' he sighed. 'I admit I was angry last night. But I can see now I was wrong. I had no right to question you.'

'Yes, you *did*!' she insisted.

'No, Audrey. You were right. I was wrong. End of argument. You go to your appointment and I'll see you when you get home tonight, fair enough?'

She fell silent, feeling totally frustrated.

'Audrey?'

'Yes?' she snapped.

He sighed again. 'Now *I've* got a headache. Perhaps it's just as well you're not coming home for lunch.'

'Perhaps it is,' she grumped, and hung up.

Oh, God, she thought, and closed her eyes. Now why did I do that? She shook her head and stared down at her shaking hands. When she looked up Edward was watching her, a rueful expression in his eyes.

Audrey arrived back at the office shortly before two, armed with the knowledge that she was as healthy as a horse and would live till she was a hundred. The doctor's words, not hers.

'If I feel as rotten as this all the time,' she muttered aloud as she dropped her handbag beside her desk, 'I won't even want to live till I'm thirty.'

Edward jumped to his feet from behind his desk and strode out of his glassed-in cubicle. 'That's it! I have no hope of concentrating on this sales budget with you muttering away like that.' He came over and thumped the top of her desk. 'Besides, life's too short to ruin what little you have of it. Now get out of here. Go home or wherever that erstwhile lover of yours is and make up with him. That's an order!'

Audrey was startled for a moment, but then excited. Edward was right! That was exactly what she should do. Go home and make up. What did it matter if Elliot only wanted sex from her for now? Maybe in time things would change. Why spoil what they had going for them by trying to rush things?

With a sincere thank you and goodbye, Audrey hurried down to where her red Magna was parked in the street, only to grind to a halt when she spied Russell leaning with casual menace against the driver's door.

'I knew I'd catch up with you if I waited here long enough,' came his snarled remark as she continued a reluctant approach, her heart racing. 'Though it's rather hard to recognise the new Audrey from the plain little piece of a few weeks ago. Not that it makes any real difference...' His lips curled sneeringly. 'You could glam yourself up till the cows came home, honey, and you'd still be the most boring screw in the world!'

A furious heat zoomed into her cheeks, anger replacing any feelings of fear. 'Move out of my way, Russell. I have no intention of standing here, listening to insults.'

'Really? And what are you going to do about it? Have me fired again?'

'I didn't have you fired,' she bit out.

'Sure you did, sweetheart. But do you know what? You did me a favour. I've landed a fantastic job as a sales manager in New Guinea, starting next week. Still, I just couldn't leave without letting you in on a little secret of mine.' His mouth pulled back into a malicious smile. 'Diane wasn't the only piece I had on the side, you know. I sampled your stepmother too. Yeah...the sexy Lavinia... Now there's a woman who knows how to please a man. My, you've gone a bit pale, ducky. Is your new playboy lover looking in that direction already?' His laughter was grotesque. 'I'll just bet he is. Why don't you ask him what he gets up to while you're at work?'

'Get out of my way!' Audrey cried, and shoved him violently to one side. He didn't try to stop her from getting in and driving off, a quick glance in the rear-view mirror showing him still standing there, laughing at her.

Audrey's hands shook on the wheel all the way home. She almost sobbed with relief as the car shot up Elliot's steep driveway. All she could think was having him hold her, comfort her, reassure her. But her relief was to be short-lived, changed to a jolting shock when she spicd a palc mauve Fiat parked beside the black Saab in Elliot's garage. Every drop of blood drained from her face and she braked to an unsteady halt.

Lavinia drove a pale mauve Fiat. Not a very common colour or make.

No, she thought, and was almost sick on the spot. No...

Somehow she climbed out of her car and walked past the Fiat to stare up at the internal staircase and the closed door at the top. But she couldn't go in that way, so tcrrified was she of what she might find if she walked in, unannounced. Instead she made her way round to the wooden staircase that led up to an entrance at the side of the house, each step an agony for her.

Once in front of the solid wooden door, Audrey rang the doorbell, then held the railing behind her for support as the seconds ticked away. What was Elliot doing, she agonised, that he wouldn't or *couldn't* answer the door straight away?

But in the end the door *was* reefed open, and her Elliot stood there, his hair mussed, a scarlet silk dressing-gown over nothing but the bottom half of a pair of scarlet silk pyjamas.

Her mind struggled to find some excuse, some reason for what she was seeing before her. But once she witnessed the guilty fluster on Elliot's face she sank into utter despair.

'God, Audrey, you said you weren't coming home till tonight.'

'*Audrey*?' she heard Lavinia gasp from somewhere behind him.

'What are you *doing* here?' he demanded, almost angrily.

'I came home early to make up,' she said in an empty voice. 'I see I shouldn't have.'

'It's not what you're thinking, dammit!'

She laughed. It sounded like glass breaking. 'My father has a saying. If an animal looks like a dog, sounds like a dog and smells like a dog, then you can be pretty sure it's a dog.' Devastated eyes raked over his undressed state before she whirled and bolted down the stairs.

'Come back!' he yelled after her.

She was too fast for him. Far too fast. For one thing, her keys were still in the ignition. She leapt into the Magna, fired the engine and backed up, executing a reverse spin with sheer luck rather than skill, then screeching off down the drive.

Tears blurred her vision but the traffic was light and she had no trouble putting distance between herself and any pursuer. Or so she thought. But as she was slowing down for a red light at the bottom of a hill, she spotted Elliot's black Saab in the rear-view mirror coming over the crest, closing fast.

The red light changed to green at the last second and she shot forward, but simultaneously the driver of a four-wheel-drive vehicle decided to run the red light the opposite way. A collision was unavoidable, Audrey's brown eyes flaring wide with fear as she saw the vehicle bearing down upon her.

She didn't scream for long, the impact throwing her forward, her forehead hitting the steering-wheel, cracking her head and pitching her into a painless black nothingness at one and the same time.

Bystanders were to tell the tale later of a black car pulling up seconds after the accident and a crazed man in a red silk dressing-gown leaping out to race over to the crushed red sedan. They said they would never forget the look in his eyes when he failed to open the crumpled door, or his desperation as he screamed for someone to ring the rescue squad and ambulance, or the way he eventually sank to his knees on the ground beside the woman driver's door and cried like a baby.

# CHAPTER TWELVE

'No.' AUDREY turned her face away from her father to stare blankly across the hospital room.

'Audrey...aren't you *ever* going to listen to reason? Nothing happened between Elliot and Lavinia that day. Even *I* believe that. Oh, I'm not saying she wouldn't have gone to bed with him if she'd been able to seduce him. She admits it. But Elliot would have none of her!'

Audrey's head turned slowly back on the pillow. 'Sure...' Her eyes were dead. 'That's why he was half naked.'

'But he said he can *explain* that, if only you'll let him. Why won't you see him?'

Audrey closed her eyes, her mind unwillingly drawn back to the day a week ago when she'd been well enough to have visitors, and Elliot and Lavinia had come into her room to see her, together. She had taken one look at them both and been consumed with the most unbearable pain. Everything had seemed to explode in her head and she'd become quite hysterical, so much so that her doctor had forbidden them entry again.

Lavinia hadn't tried to return. Elliot had not been so easy to turn away.

He'd come back the next day and argued with the doctor vehemently till he was allowed into her room, though only with the doctor in tow. Audrey had heard the vocal confrontation in the corridor outside her door, giving her time to cloak her distress within a hard shell of bitter resolve. But when Elliot actually walked in, she'd been momentarily startled by his ghastly state. My God, he'd looked like he hadn't slept for a week!

But she had quickly dismissed any pity and hardened her heart, deciding he was only suffering from guilt. When he'd started to speak, Audrey had looked right through him and told the doctor if her unwelcome visitor didn't leave immediately she would get out of her bed and leave the room herself. Since she was recovering from surgery on a broken hip and several crushed ribs, her threat was not to be taken lightly.

When she had started to move her legs sideways under the sheet, Elliot had left. But he hadn't given up.

He'd tried ringing.

She hung up on him without saying a word.

He'd sent flowers and letters.

She sent the flowers down to the children's ward and burnt the letters, watching the paper curling up into blackened ash.

Audrey knew she would never believe anything Elliot had to say. It was all too clear in her mind. His undressed state. His guilty fluster. The incredible coincidence of Lavinia being there on the one and only day she hadn't come home for lunch.

The only thing that puzzled her was why Elliot was trying to secure her understanding and forgiveness at all. If he was prepared to go to bed with the likes of Lavinia then he had no conscience anyway.

'Audrey...'

She snapped back to the present, realising her father was still sitting next to her. 'Yes?'

'Hear the man out.'

'No.' Her tone was implacable and her father rose wearily to his feet.

'You're just like your mother. She was stubborn too, wouldn't listen when I tried to undo the malicious gossip of some old biddy who'd told her I'd married her for her money.'

'*Hadn't* you?' Audrey said flatly.

'Yes ... But your mother didn't know that, and by the time this gossip did its mischief I'd long really fallen in love with her. We had a good marriage. We'd been happy, especially after you came along. But she wouldn't listen to me, wouldn't look beyond the obvious to the real truth. She threw away the rest of our lives together and made my personal life hell. She refused to sleep with me and in the end I turned to Lavinia for comfort. Don't do what she did, Audrey. Don't cut off your nose to spite your face. Elliot loves you. I'll bet my boots on it!'

Yvonne said as much to her the following afternoon when she came to visit. 'I can see the situation with Elliot and that woman must have looked very bad,' she said bluntly. 'But Audrey ... Elliot assures me he's innocent and I believe him. My dear, if only you could have seen him during the days after your accident when you were in a coma from concussion. He was beside himself! He didn't sleep, didn't eat. Do you know what you're doing to him, refusing even to see him? He doesn't know where to turn, what to do. In desperation he's asked me to give you a message, to tell you that he's not a Russell, whatever that means!'

Audrey flinched. For the concept of putting Elliot in the same category as Russell was simply impossible. Finally, she was forced to face a remote possibility. Maybe she was wrong about Elliot. Maybe he had been the victim of circumstance, or Lavinia's manipulations. Maybe...

'Think about it, my dear,' Yvonne said more gently. 'If you don't give Elliot a chance to explain, won't you always wonder if you'd made a big mistake? You love Elliot. But love is never enough to build a future on. You must have trust as well.'

Audrey's heart twisted. Trust... That was all very well to say, but there was a fine line between trust and naïveté. Elliot's message did not mention love and she could not afford to make another monumental mistake. Not if she valued her mental health.

'I...I will think about it, Yvonne. Thank you. You've been very kind, coming to visit all the time.'

'My pleasure. Well, I must be going now. I'll be back to see you tomorrow and we'll talk some more.'

'I'd like that. You're a good friend.'

Audrey was lying there quietly, thinking about what Yvonne had said, when there was a tap on her door. She glanced up just in time to see Lavinia walk into the room.

Audrey's whole chest tightened, every fibre of her being reacting violently. Her feelings must have shown on her face for Lavinia stayed well away from her bed, looking distraught herself. 'Please don't send me away,' she blurted out. 'I...I *have* to talk to you.'

Perhaps it was the real tears swimming in Lavinia's eyes that softened Audrey's heart. Or the fact that her stepmother didn't look like herself at all. She was almost...unkempt, her hair in disarray, no make-up on, her yellow linen suit quite crumpled.

Audrey couldn't find it in her heart to send her away. But she couldn't speak, either. In the end, Lavinia gingerly approached the foot of the bed.

'I...don't know where to start,' she sobbed, and looked down at the floor. Tears ran down her cheeks and dripped from her nose. 'You must hate me. *Everyone* hates me. Everyone except Warwick. He's been...amazingly caring and understanding.'

'He loves you,' Audrey managed to say.

'Yes,' Lavinia nodded. 'I can see that now. I never thought he did. I thought...' She shook her head. 'The day we were married he told me he didn't want children. I was crushed. I wanted a child. But all Warwick seemed to need from me was sex. I used to think it was because he wasn't capable of loving anyone after your mother's death. He even sent you off to boarding-school. But then I saw how he so looked forward to your coming home in the holidays and I was deeply jealous. I hated the place you held in his heart,' Lavinia confessed unhappily.

'You shouldn't have, Lavinia,' Audrey said kindly. 'I used to think Father didn't love me at all. I only realised recently that he finds it hard to show his love, to be demonstrative.'

'Yes, so he's been telling me, but I too thought he didn't love me, especially when as the years went by he seemed to withdraw further from me. Sex became less important to him. He found other interests, golf and collecting art. I felt...neglected. I...I did things...Things I deeply regret.'

Audrey's stomach turned over. Russell, she thought. She's talking about Russell...

'When you started blossoming and then produced Elliot, I was green with envy. I...I went really crazy. I wanted to strike out at you, and Warwick. I thought if I got Elliot to go to bed with me I would soothe this devil that was raging within me. But Elliot didn't touch me, Audrey. I swear it! Don't ever doubt he loves you. He does. Very deeply. I don't think he realised how much till all this happened. *I'm* to blame for everything, your break-up with Elliot, your accident. You *have* to believe me!'

Audrey stared into those wild black eyes, full of such pain and remorse, and finally saw the truth. It hit her like a physical blow. 'I do, Lavinia. I *do*.'

'Oh, thank God,' she cried. 'Thank God. Maybe now I'll be able to live with myself at last.'

'Lavinia?' Audrey said shakily, her heart racing. 'Yes?'

'Would you mind leaving me now? There's something I have to do...'

'Oh... Yes, of course. Thank you again, Audrey, for listening to me. I hope that some day you might find it in your heart to forgive me too.'

The moment Lavinia left the room, Audrey snatched up the phone next to her bed, her hands trembling as she dialled.

'Elliot Knight speaking,' he answered on the third ring.

Audrey sucked in a silent gasp. How dreadful he sounded. So lifeless and dull. Not like her Elliot at all.

Her heart groaned with regret. I've done this to him, me and my stupid lack of trust. Only an innocent man suffered like this. Only an innocent man would have persisted after being so cruelly rejected. Oh, how blind I've been!

'Elliot?'

The silence at the other end was like a dagger in her heart. She could feel Elliot's torment like a tangible thing, piercing into her soul.

'Elliot, I'm so sorry,' she cried. 'I know you didn't do anything wrong. Forgive me for ever doubting you. I...please come in and see me.'

She waited breathlessly for him to speak but still he was silent. Or so she thought. But when his voice finally came down the line, choked with emotion, she knew he'd been struggling to regain his composure. 'I'll be there as soon as I can,' he rasped.

It took him twenty minutes, no doubt another record since the Royal North Shore Hospital was hardly on Newport's doorstep. Audrey had planned how she would greet him, with warm smiles and loving words. Instead she took one look at his ravaged face and darkly ringed eyes and burst into tears.

Elliot looked shattered for a moment. But then he came forward to sink down beside her bed and gather her into his arms. 'Oh, Audrey,' he groaned. 'My darling...my sweetest love...'

They just held each other for a long long time. Several nurses peeped in, and went away, smiling happily.

'It's just as well dear old Russell's gone to New Guinea,' Elliot said a long time later. 'Because if he hadn't I'd pulverise the bastard! No wonder you jumped to the conclusions you did, after what he said to you.'

'I still should have given you a chance to explain,' Audrey murmured, 'how you were half-dressed that day because you went back to bed with a migraine.'

Elliot nodded. 'Once I took some pain-killers I was soon out like a light. I was sound asleep when Lavinia knocked and I didn't have enough presence of mind not to let her in. Besides, she pretended she was concerned about you and wanted to see if you were all right. I didn't ask her to come, Audrey.'

'I know that now, but it was such an amazing coincidence, her showing up on the one day I didn't come home for lunch.'

'It was no coincidence. Edward had mentioned the staff medicals when he'd been at Warwick's for drinks at the weekend. She knew exactly where you'd be. When she started trying to seduce me, I really took her to task, told her she should wake up to herself before Warwick divorced her. Then I hauled her over the coals over her treatment of you. By the time you arrived, I think my words were beginning to sink in. She seemed genuinely upset. But after your accident she really cracked up. Lavinia is a very remorseful woman, believe me.'

'I know. She came to see me. But it wasn't only her so much who opened my eyes. It was Yvonne...'

'Aaah.... She gave you my message, did she, about my not being a Russell?'

'Yes. How I could have ever believed you could act like him I don't know.'

'I wasn't always so noble, Audrey. But I've changed.'

'Moira changed you,' she said simply.

Elliot was taken aback. 'Why do you say that? What do you know about Moira?'

'Yvonne told me a lot about Moira. And about you.'

'*Me*? She knows very little about me!'

'Doesn't she? She was a close friend of Moira's, Elliot. Women friends confide in each other. Women don't have to put on a macho show, like men. They can open up to each other without fear of being ridiculed, or thought less of.'

His grey eyes clouded over with deep thought. 'That must be quite something,' he murmured.

'You can always open up to me, Elliot,' she said gently. 'That's what true love is all about. You need never feel alone, never keep deep dark secrets.'

He stared at her for a long time, his eyes deeply thoughtful. Then he picked up her hand and spoke in a low measured voice.

'In that case, there is something I'd like to tell you, to explain my past attitude to love.'

'Yes?'

'There was this girl once...'

Audrey tried not to look startled. A girl? He couldn't possibly be talking about Moira here.

'She was rich...beautiful...sexy...I was twenty-two at the time. It was my first year on the European skiing circuit. Felicity was her name, and following the ski-season her game. Only I didn't know that at the time. I fell madly in love with her. She told me she really loved me back and wanted to know everything about me. I've never liked talking about my past but she kept on and on at me till it all came out, about my——'

His eyes snapped up. 'Did Yvonne tell you about my childhood, and my...mother?'

Audrey nodded. 'I know she was an alcoholic and abandoned you when you were eight. I also know about the foster homes and the institution...'

For a second Elliot looked annoyed, but then he nodded too, a wry smile softening his annoyance. 'Moira always was a sticky-beak into people's pasts. She thought their past held the key to their future. Not an excuse, but a key...'

A very smart woman, your Moira, Audrey thought.

'Anyway, I was too dumb to notice Felicity's withdrawal when she found out I'd been a charity case. When she didn't come to my room the next night I went in search of her. I found her all right...'

There was no denying the black cynicism in Elliot's voice.

'In bed with another man?'

'Not quite. In bed with *two* other men.'

Audrey cringed with disgust.

'Yes. Not a pretty picture. She didn't even know I came and went, she was so—er—busy.'

'Oh, Elliot. I can see that must have made you very bitter about love and women.'

'Partly. But that's not the point of the story.'

'I...I don't understand.'

'I realised very quickly, you see, that I'd never loved Felicity at all, that my feelings had been entirely sexual. She was my first woman, you see. Unfortunately, my cold reaction to Felicity's disloyalty only reinforced what I already suspected about myself. That I was a hard bastard who'd had every scrap of real love and caring torn out of me during my younger years. After that, I plunged into a life of transitory sexual relationships, never turning a hair when each was over. It wasn't till I met Moira that I realised I could actually be friends with a woman.'

He smiled a rueful, remembering smile. 'Do you know, she actually said that, if I was such a black-hearted rogue, then why did I only have affairs with the sort of older woman whose hearts wouldn't be too badly broken? Of course I told her she was crazy, that I was rotten through and through. At which she only laughed and suggested that in that case I should move in with her so that she could salvage my soul.'

'Which she did...'

Elliot shook his head. 'No, Audrey. Moira didn't salvage me at all. While I was married to her I still did exactly what I liked, when I liked, my only concession to my marriage being that I gave up sleeping with other women. I hurt her, Audrey, with my aloofness, my indifference. For Moira truly loved me. She told me just before she died. It...rather broke me up. And made me vow never to hurt anyone like that again...'

He closed his eyes briefly and shook his head. 'But I did... With you...' He heaved a ragged sigh. 'Hell, I tried not to. I came home after dropping you off that first Friday night and broke the world record for long cold showers. And what did you do? Called me up, conned me into seeing you again then showed up looking like a goddess. I kept telling myself hands off, but somehow my body didn't get the message. Nor my heart. For while I was wanting to make love to you, I also ached to cherish and protect you, to give you everything I thought you deserved. But I'd spent too many years not listening to my heart to take notice of its new message. And too many years listening to my body to ignore its very familiar demands.'

He reached out and gently touched her face. 'Yet, in a way, it was sex that showed me the difference between what I felt for you and any previous woman. In the past I could satiate my desires with frequency. But with you, Audrey... The more I made love to you, the more I wanted and needed you. You made me feel so special, my darling, so loved. If anyone has salvaged me, sweet thing, it was you... with your gloriously unselfish nature, your kind and trusting soul, your true beauty...'

He kissed her then, his lips trembling with emotion. 'It took the shock of seeing you unconscious in that car to make me wake up to myself. I prayed for your life that day, Audrey. Prayed hard. And I vowed that if God gave you back to me I would never hurt you again as long as I lived. I love you, Audrey. Love you terribly. And I want to marry you, have babies with you. Will you take a chance and say yes?'

Audrey's heart quivered with joy. 'Oh, Elliot... Yes. Yes. Oh, you've made me so happy.'

'I hope so, my darling. Because if anyone deserves to be happy you do.'

The music started up and Audrey took her father's arm, giving him a nervous but loving glance as she did so. He looked very handsome and dignified, every inch the proud father of the bride. Not to mention the proud father of a babe-to-be, Lavinia having recently announced the warming news that she was going to have a baby.

'You look so beautiful,' he whispered as they started the walk down the aisle behind the matron of honour. 'And so does your friend. That deep red is very becoming on her.'

Audrey smiled, remembering how Yvonne had initially resisted her offer to be the bridal attendant opposite Nigel as best man. 'But I'm too *old*!' she protested.

'You'd better just go along with what she wants, Yvonne,' Elliot said with a sigh. 'God knows what happened to the sweet malleable young thing I fell in love with. She's turned into a real tartar! Do you know what she told me the other day? That I had to go back to work—said she can't have the father of her children lounging around the house all day like some gigolo. Well, I ask you!'

They all laughed and Yvonne gave way.

Now the big moment had come and Audrey was drifting down the aisle, past her smiling friends and relatives, all of them giving her admiring glances. Then suddenly Yvonne turned the corner at the end of the aisle and Audrey saw Elliot, standing there, waiting for her.

Her eyes glazed and she was reliving it all—that first moment in the coffee-lounge, with her gallant knight coming to her rescue; their wonderful weekend of lovemaking down at the chalet; their long long talks which often extended well into the night nowadays; and now this... Her eyes cleared to focus on Elliot... This was the best moment of all, when they were about to pledge themselves to each other forever.

She reached him and he took her hand, smiling down at her with so much love in his face. 'Not nervous, are you?' he asked softly.

'No.'

'I love you.'

'I love you, too...'

The minister coughed, then began to speak. 'We are gathered here together in the sight of God ... to join together this man and this woman in holy matrimony...'

Bystanders were to tell the tale for years afterwards of the wedding they had witnessed between the strikingly handsome groom and delicately fair bride, of the way they looked at each other during the ceremony, and how, by the time the minister pronounced them man and wife, there was hardly a dry eye in the church.

# IT'S FREE! IT'S FUN! ENTER THE

## ☆ "Hooray for ☆ ☆ Hollywood" ☆

### SWEEPSTAKES!

**W**e're giving away prizes to celebrate the screening of four new romance movies on CBS TV this fall! Look for the movies on four Sunday afternoons in October. And be sure to return your Official Entry Coupons to try for a fabulous **vacation in Hollywood!**

 If you're the Grand Prize winner we'll fly you and your companion to Los Angeles for a 7-day/6-night vacation you'll never forget!

 You'll stay at the luxurious Regent Beverly Wilshire Hotel,* a prime location for celebrity spotting!

 You'll have time to visit Universal Studios,* stroll the Hollywood Walk of Fame, check out celebrities' footprints at Mann's Chinese Theater, ride a trolley to see the homes of the stars, and more!

 The prize includes a rental car for 7 days and $1,000.00 pocket money!

**Someone's** going to win this fabulous prize, and it might just be you! Remember, the more times you enter, the better your chances of winning!

 † Five hundred entrants will each receive SUNGLASSES OF THE STARS! Don't miss out. ENTER TODAY!

The proprietors of the trademark are not associated with this promotion.

# Take 4 bestselling love stories FREE

## Plus get a FREE surprise gift!

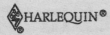

# "HOORAY FOR HOLLYWOOD" SWEEPSTAKES

# HERE'S HOW THE SWEEPSTAKES WORKS

## OFFICIAL RULES — NO PURCHASE NECESSARY

To enter, complete an Official Entry Form or hand print on a 3" x 5" card the words "HOORAY FOR HOLLYWOOD", your name and address and mail your entry in the pre-addressed envelope (if provided) or to: "Hooray for Hollywood" Sweepstakes, P.O. Box 9076, Buffalo, NY 14269-9076 or "Hooray for Hollywood" Sweepstakes, P.O. Box 637, Fort Erie, Ontario L2A 5X3. Entries must be sent via First Class Mail and be received no later than 12/31/94. No liability is assumed for lost, late or misdirected mail.

Winners will be selected in random drawings to be conducted no later than January 31, 1995 from all eligible entries received.

Grand Prize: A 7-day/6-night trip for 2 to Los Angeles, CA including round trip air transportation from commercial airport nearest winner's residence, accommodations at the Regent Beverly Wilshire Hotel, free rental car, and $1,000 spending money. (Approximate prize value which will vary dependent upon winner's residence: $5,400.00 U.S.); 500 Second Prizes: A pair of "Hollywood Star" sunglasses (prize value: $9.95 U.S. each). Winner selection is under the supervision of D.L. Blair, Inc., an independent judging organization, whose decisions are final. Grand Prize travelers must sign and return a release of liability prior to traveling. Trip must be taken by 2/1/96 and is subject to airline schedules and accommodations availability.

Sweepstakes offer is open to residents of the U.S. (except Puerto Rico) and Canada who are 18 years of age or older, except employees and immediate family members of Harlequin Enterprises, Ltd., its affiliates, subsidiaries, and all agencies, entities or persons connected with the use, marketing or conduct of this sweepstakes. All federal, state, provincial, municipal and local laws apply. Offer void wherever prohibited by law. Taxes and/or duties are the sole responsibility of the winners. Any litigation within the province of Quebec respecting the conduct and awarding of prizes may be submitted to the Regie des loteries et courses du Quebec. All prizes will be awarded; winners will be notified by mail. No substitution of prizes are permitted. Odds of winning are dependent upon the number of eligible entries received.

Potential grand prize winner must sign and return an Affidavit of Eligibility within 30 days of notification. In the event of non-compliance within this time period, prize may be awarded to an alternate winner. Prize notification returned as undeliverable may result in the awarding of prize to an alternate winner. By acceptance of their prize, winners consent to use of their names, photographs, or likenesses for purpose of advertising, trade and promotion on behalf of Harlequin Enterprises, Ltd., without further compensation unless prohibited by law. A Canadian winner must correctly answer an arithmetical skill-testing question in order to be awarded the prize.

For a list of winners (available after 2/28/95), send a separate stamped, self-addressed envelope to: Hooray for Hollywood Sweepstakes 3252 Winners, P.O. Box 4200, Blair, NE 68009.

CBSRLS

## OFFICIAL ENTRY COUPON

# "Hooray for Hollywood"
### SWEEPSTAKES!

Yes, I'd love to win the Grand Prize — a vacation in Hollywood —
or one of 500 pairs of "sunglasses of the stars"! Please enter me
in the sweepstakes!

This entry must be received by December 31, 1994.
Winners will be notified by January 31, 1995.

Name _____

Address _____ Apt. _____

City _____

State/Prov. _____ Zip/Postal Code _____

Daytime phone number _____
(area code)

Mail all entries to: Hooray for Hollywood Sweepstakes,
P.O. Box 9076, Buffalo, NY 14269-9076.
In Canada, mail to: Hooray for Hollywood Sweepstakes,
P.O. Box 637, Fort Erie, ON L2A 5X3.

KCH

---

## OFFICIAL ENTRY COUPON

# "Hooray for Hollywood"
### SWEEPSTAKES!

Yes, I'd love to win the Grand Prize — a vacation in Hollywood —
or one of 500 pairs of "sunglasses of the stars"! Please enter me
in the sweepstakes!

This entry must be received by December 31, 1994.
Winners will be notified by January 31, 1995.

Name _____

Address _____ Apt. _____

City _____

State/Prov. _____ Zip/Postal Code _____

Daytime phone number _____
(area code)

Mail all entries to: Hooray for Hollywood Sweepstakes,
P.O. Box 9076, Buffalo, NY 14269-9076.
In Canada, mail to: Hooray for Hollywood Sweepstakes,
P.O. Box 637, Fort Erie, ON L2A 5X3.

KCH